SCARLET

BOOK TWO OF THE ROBYN HOOD ADVENTURES

NIAMH MURPHY

NIM PUBLISHING

This book is a work of fiction. Any references to historical events, real people, or real places are used fictitiously. Other names, characters, places and events are products of the author's imagination, and any resemblance to actual events, places or persons, living or dead, is entirely coincidental.

Copyright © 2021 by Niamh Murphy

All rights reserved.

No part of this book may be reproduced in any form or by any electronic or mechanical means, including information storage and retrieval systems, without written permission from the author, except for the use of brief quotations in a book review.

For Louise

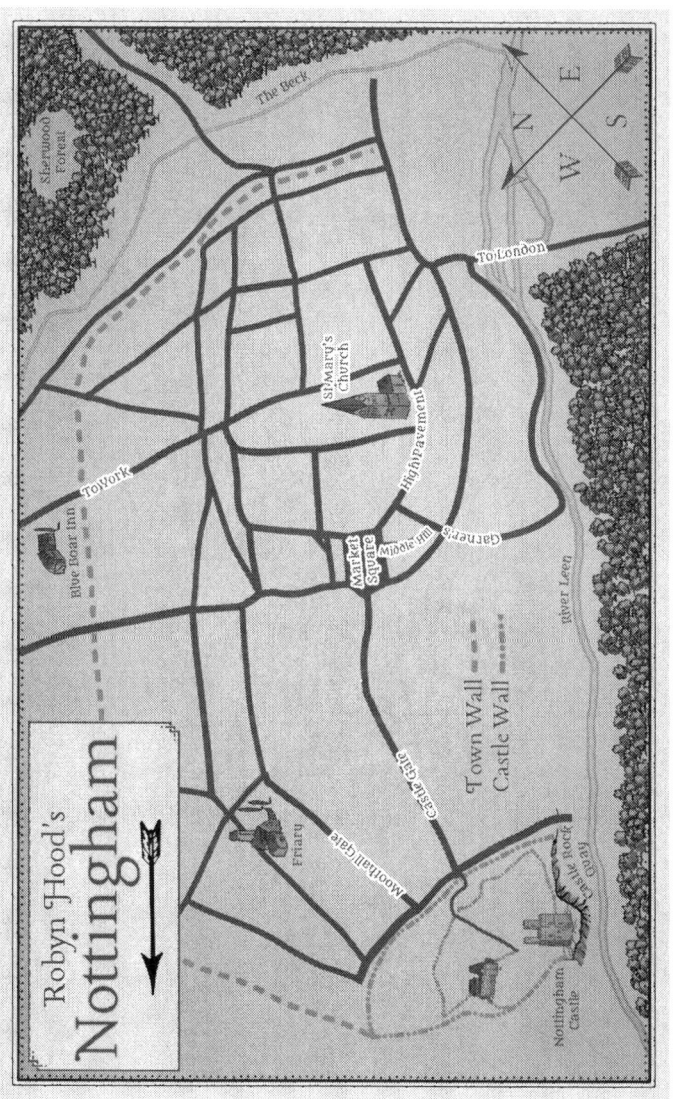

1

MICHAELMAS

Robyn watched the festivities from her seat in the corner. Her green hood was pulled up to cover her dark red hair but she had let the scarf drop from her face and tapped her foot in rhythm with the drums. Although The Blue Boar Inn was filled with friends dancing and merrymaking to the raucous music, she was still in the dangerous territory of Nottingham town.

Officially, the merrymaking was in honour of St Michael. But the garlands of ivy, decorated pinecones and three dancing Green Men were more than enough to betray the pagan harvest festival.

The travelling players were, at least, a nod to the Michaelmas fayre. They were masked and wore costumes of angels, the devil, Eve, Adam and St Michael himself complete with a wooden sword and shield. The tavern's current minstrel, a fair lad of no more than twenty, was dressed in a bright blue tunic with extravagant sleeves and faux gold trim. His eyes shone in the lantern light as he played a jig on his whistle while two grinning locals joined in with drums and lutes.

Alis, the pretty tapster, brought over another tray of cider and placed a tankard in front of Robyn, waving away a silver farthing as the outlaw went to pay.

"Not dancin' then Robyn?" she asked.

"No." Robyn shook her head as she took a sip of the crisp, golden liquid and enjoyed the effect on her tongue and on her head. "I'm not fool enough to tread on *his* toes."

She indicated the man in the middle of the floor. He was larger than the other two dancers and was made larger still by a pair of antlers on his headdress. His fierce, grinning mask was either a wodwos or the devil depending on whether it was a priest or local who asked. Dressed in heavy furs rather than garlands of green leaves like the others, he was still lighter on his feet than a maiden on May Day.

"Aye," Alis chuckled, "best no one get in Littlejohn's way while he's a leapin'."

They laughed but Robyn caught sight of Alis' father Merek, the innkeeper. He was a portly man with thinning hair and, more often than not, a cheerful countenance that easily spread to his customers; but now Merek's cheeks were red and his brow furrowed as he fought through the merry makers over to Robyn's corner.

"Guards," he hissed, patting his glistening face with a cloth.

Robyn nodded, the smile falling from her face. She wiped the cider from her lips and grabbed her bow before elbowing her way through the regulars and tugging on Littlejohn's sleeve mid twirl.

His head snapped around; a grin spread thickly across his hairy cheeks.

"Time to go," she called over the music.

His grin fell and he nodded. He performed a final

dramatic bow to rapturous applause and pleas to stay before following Robyn to the beckoning innkeeper.

"Through t'back," Merek hissed, waving frantically and looking behind them lest anyone notice their escape. He led them into the darkened storeroom crammed ceiling-high with wooden barrels and dried meats that hung from the rafters. As he opened a shutter, the late afternoon light spilt into the room and Robyn was surprised it was still so early.

She thanked Merek profusely for his hospitality as she slid over the sill and out into the yard.

"Yes, yes, yes," he hissed frantically, waving her off. Littlejohn scrambled through after her, losing his headdress on the way and leaning back in for it. "Be off with ye!" Merek could barely seal the shutters behind them fast enough and Robyn wondered just how close their escape had been.

The pair slid through the yard to peer around the corner of the building. Two armed men dressed in the red livery with the green cross and crowns of Nottingham and wearing the grim mood of the overworked and underfed, were tending to their horses in the main yard of The Blue Boar Inn.

Robyn turned to Littlejohn, a finger to her lips. He nodded.

"Welcome! Welcome, gentlemen!" Although feigning the refined Norman accent, Robyn knew it was Merek who enthusiastically greeted the guards from the door. He would be there open-armed, a forced smile drawn over his lips. "Come in, come in, my friends," the Nottingham guards exchanged a look, then moved out of sight, "you must have some cider or perhaps my finest mead?" Their conversation was cut off at the sound of a door closing with a thud and Robyn let out a long, deep sigh and nodded to Littlejohn.

Keeping low, she opened the little wicker-gate of the yard and slipped through.

Scampering across narrow paths, and diving down back alleys, Robyn and Littlejohn made their way through the higgledy-piggledy collection of hovels and cattle houses that made up the cheapest part of Nottingham town. Not even part of Nottingham proper, the poor people who lived in these streets were shut out of the main town's gates and not provided with the protection of living within the town's defences. Yet these narrow, wattle-lined paths were still regularly patrolled by the sheriff's guards who looked out for any reason to charge a fine or two.

It wasn't until the pair were safely beyond the northern lavender fields, green after their late summer plucking, that Robyn felt confident enough to lower her guard and enjoy the warmth of the cider on her senses and the sun on her back.

She smiled in relief and quiet joy, her purse was far lighter than when they had made the journey that morning although neither of them had paid for a morsel of food or a sip of cider.

"Today was a good day, was it not my friend?" Robyn grinned, looking up at her friend and thinking of the people of the poor district who, thanks to Robyn and Littlejohn, had paid their rent on time and in full for the first time in years.

Littlejohn's curling black hair was matted and damp from having spent the best part of the day under his thick headdress of furs and antlers. His cheeks were reddened under his unkempt beard and his eyes were bloodshot after a morning spent on cider. In one hand he clutched his precious headdress while in the other, he held a strong wooden stave. It was a weapon he fought well with, although today the merry man needed it more to keep him on his feet.

"Aye," he agreed with a happy sigh, "T'was not a bad day."

They made their way up the path toward the line of trees that marked the edge of the King's Forest of Sherwood. Hundreds of acres of rich green woodland that gave the pair much-needed cover to evade the law. The high sheriff of Nottinghamshire and Derbyshire had been searching for Robyn for more than a month but there was little chance he would ever find her in the thousands of acres of forest.

"Halt, who goes there?"

Robyn turned, dumbfounded. Happily prattling on to Littlejohn, neither of them had heard the approach of three mounted soldiers. The men wore pointed helms, chainmail, and an unknown livery of gold and red quartered, with a white star emblazoned on the chest. But it was the sharp pikes pointed directly at her head that startled Robyn.

"Answer me, boy." The demand came from a heavy-set man, with young eyes, but a well-groomed beard of pure white, who seemed to oversee the others. He peered down at her awaiting her excuses but Robyn's mouth merely opened and closed, unable to conjure an answer.

"Foresters," Littlejohn managed quickly, only the slightest slur in his speech, "we're just after the Feast o' St Michael, sire. On our way home now."

The man glanced at the trees and looked back at them. "So, you got yourselves merry and fancied yourselves a little bit of poaching of the king's deer, did you?"

"Nay, sire!" Littlejohn shook `his head furiously and Robyn joined him, suddenly remembering to secure her scarf over the lower half of her face. "We're just honest men, never touched a deer in our lives, have we lad?"

"Nay, not poachers, sire!" Robyn assured them, lowering her voice a little unconvincingly.

"So, those antlers just fell off a passing stag, did they?" The soldier leaned forward, and even under his helmet, Robyn could see the man's eyebrows rise in incredulity.

"Ah," Littlejohn glanced down at his headdress for a long moment. "Scarper!" He shouted, then turned and darted for the trees. It took just half a second for Robyn to tear after him and the sound of crashing hooves took only half a moment longer.

As Littlejohn darted to the left, Robyn took a sharp right, then a left, and a right again, darting in and out of trees, and leaping branches and ditches.

Their pursuers had horses but in the forest that was little advantage. Robyn could turn in an instant and dart between trees, squeeze through bushes, and duck under branches. If they could keep their wits about them, the pair could shake off their pursuers and meet up back at camp.

Her face was hot, her stomach heavy after feasting, and her head foggy after the drink. She pulled off her scarf, gulping in the cool air as she made a quick feint to the left before leaping into a low, dry gully and dashing to the right. She could still hear the pounding of hooves. *Where were they?*

Foolishly, she glanced behind as she ran catching sight of the gold and red livery of her pursuer. She wobbled, her foot caught and she crashed to the ground.

Robyn didn't have a moment to dwell on her bruises, instead, she scrambled to her feet, nocked an arrow, and launched it blindly at her pursuer. He caught it on his shield, barely pausing as he charged at her, his pike at the ready. Leaping out of the way of the charge, Robyn clattered to the hard, dry earth for a second time as the mounted guard raced past. Her blood pounded in her chest and the beating of her heart was almost all she could hear.

Crouched, her eyes scanning the woods, Robyn clutched her bow, making ready to run. Where the devil did he go? She could hear her pursuer but couldn't place him.

Then, too late for her to leap from its path, the horse and rider were galloping toward her. Blind panic took over and she grabbed the soldier's pike sidestepping as they charged at her and wrenching it from the man's grasp. Less than an inch between her and death.

Shocked, she stared at the weapon for a moment. By rights the thing should have pierced right through her chest. In disgust, she threw the accursed weapon aside and took off in the opposite direction.

But she was out of breath and bruised. She had to admit her senses were dulled by the festival and, rather than a dashing escape, Robyn blundered and scrambled through the woods; her breathing heavier and louder than church bells at Christmas.

Her path was cut off before she had made it more than a few feet. A new guard or the same guard, she didn't know, all she saw was the horse rearing and the axe blade raised.

In a lightning flash of instinct, her bow was ready and raised. But he was too close. The instant the arrow was released he brought his axe down hard and heavy smashing clean through her bow. It was all she could do to dive to the ground in a rain of shattering debris.

The horse snorted, rearing for another pass, and Robyn could raise nothing but her arms to defend herself. In that instant, she knew there was nothing she could do to avoid being trampled by the beast.

But the pain never arrived. She heard a roar and a crash. But nothing followed.

Peering out from between her forearms she saw the horse; riderless.

She leapt to her feet scanning the trees just in time to witness Littlejohn crash his stave into the fallen man's head. He slumped back to the ground.

Breathing hard, Littlejohn turned to her. "You alive, rabbit?"

She nodded slowly, her heart beating a thousand times a second as she searched around for any other unseen pursuer.

But the woods were quiet and her breath returned.

She reached down to grab her bow and moaned in fresh agony. Her precious weapon lay in two pieces on the forest floor, held together only by the string. She lifted it up and wailed, "He broke my bow!"

"Aye? Well, be glad he didn't break your head." Littlejohn leaned on his stave and, noticing an axe struck into it, removed the weapon and threw it down heavily onto the unmoving man. "Who are these devils? Do you know these colours?"

Robyn shook her head, staring at the gold and red tabard that covered the man's mail. "It's not a noble family from these parts." They were well trained, fierce and possessed armour and weapons good enough for the king's own retinue; she didn't like the idea of facing any more of them.

A bugle sounded, far off to the west. The fallen soldier groaned.

"We'd best be off," Littlejohn said, "his friends shall find him soon enough."

Robyn took one last look at the soldier, wondering where these mysterious men had come from, then followed.

2

A PRINCELY DEBT

Rain drenched the earth and darkened the castle walls. Water drummed against the window shutters of William de Wendenal's study as he sat at his desk staring at the quarterly costs of Nottingham Castle. His white-knuckled hand gripped a chunk of black hair at his scalp.

"How is it the same as last quarter?" he whined his words through gritted teeth and looked up at his pale, dark-eyed wife.

Maud rolled her eyes. "If you expected a miracle William, you've been praying to the wrong saint."

"But we have fewer men."

Maud leaned on the desk, looming over his hunched figure. "Fewer men working for double wages," she hit the table, "If I have told you once, I have told you a thousand times! Cut their shifts and halve their fees. Why do we need two men at every door? Two men guarding the gaol? Two men patrolling the walls? Do they guard each other?"

William leaned back with a sigh and closed his eyes. "If I cut their wages, they will leave-"

"Nonsense."

"I lost six men to Ranulf de Staynton just this week. The Baron of Edgerton has been sniffing around making offers to the best officers."

But Maud shook her head. "Harvest has finished, there's a glut of men."

"There won't be a glut of men for as long as this damnable crusade continues."

"This 'damnable crusade' is the reason you are the sheriff. Now listen William, if we don't find that thousand silver-"

"I know, I know. I have received another letter from Prince John asking after the promise." He waved a hand irritably and stood from his desk walking over to the empty hearth. A thousand silver was enough to pay the wages of two good men for more than a year. It was money he could little afford to part with. "Why did you have to tell him we could give so much?"

"Because we had it!" Her voice rose, becoming its most shrill and William immediately regretted speaking. "We had it in our hands, William, we even sent it! And that accursed murderer stole it. A murderer you ought to have seen hanged by now."

William's jaw clenched. He hissed his reply through gritted teeth. "If I had more men I would have captured Robyn Hood by now."

"You did have more men William, and still that boy slipped through your fingers like an eel, and now the prince will either see your position is sold or have you killed." There was fire in Maud's dark eyes, but it seemed to go out as she slumped into a chair and sighed. "More likely both if he's his father's son," she added in a dry whisper.

A sharp knock at the door freed William from his duty to make a reply. "Come."

A young man with sandy hair and a poor attempt at a moustache entered. "A barge has arrived at the Castle Quay, sire, and a retinue of men leading a covered wagon make haste to the castle gates."

Maud and William glanced at one another, she was now as pale as he. "Prince John?" asked William.

But the young guard shook his head. "Nay sire, talk from quayside says it's clergy."

"Clergy?" William felt a twist in his stomach. "Not-not the Chancellor?" He looked to Maud but she raised her eyebrows in bewilderment, and William nodded to the young guard. "Prepare the men."

The guard nodded and was gone. William and Maud barely had time to gather suitable cloaks and interrogate one another about who their guest might be before the call at the main gate informed them that the mysterious caravan had arrived.

The pair rushed down to the castle ballium to be greeted by a huge retinue of impressive mounts and well-trained men making their way up the path toward the castle tower. At least two dozen riders were fitted out in costly mail armour, polished helmets, and gold and red quartered livery with a white star emblazoned on their chests. A long wagon followed behind them drawn by four white horses and covered with a fine cloth woven with golden thread. It slowly rumbled up the winding castle path and through the gates of the inner castle wall toward them.

William glanced around, the few men he had left looked shabby and tired, some were too young, most were too old, and they were all unkempt and unshaven. He too was unshaven, and the bright blue cap he'd thrust upon his head did not complement the dark green tunic he wore under his mantle.

They made for a very poor welcome.

He was relieved that his wife at least was resplendent in her long, burgundy gown and surcoat, with wide sleeves and a gold-trimmed headband atop her starched veil and dark eyes.

The long, expensive covered wagon wheeled into the courtyard, circling the flagstones before finally coming to a stop in front of them. The riders halted as one and two men leapt from their mounts and rushed to the back of the wagon. A set of wooden steps were placed on the ground by one of the men while the other pulled a cord and drew back a pair of richly embroidered curtains covering the opening at the rear.

There was a long moment of silence. No one moved. William resisted the urge to step closer and peer into the darkness beyond the curtains wondering if the inhabitant was asleep... or dead.

But finally, there was a deep groan, and a silk-slippered foot emerged, followed by the gold-trimmed hem of a long, red tunic, and the bulbous body of a man whose rounded stomach pressed at his silks. His skin was ashen, and his eyes were sunken and shadowed. The tufts of white hair that poked out from under his bishop's mitre were flecked with a dark grey and he was unsteady on his feet for a moment before pulling out a gilded stick of office upon which he leaned heavily.

The man squinted around blindly at the gathered bodies as a manservant quickly offered him a fur-lined surcoat to keep off the cold wind that pulled at his robes and exposed his swollen ankles.

"Nottingham?" It was a gruff voice thick with sleep.

William hesitated and glanced at his wife before moving forward to greet their ecclesiastical guest. "Welcome, your grace, Welcome! I trust you had a good journey?"

The bishop searched with his cloudy eyes before finding William. He reached out a thick, reddened hand and William took it eagerly, kneeling low and reluctantly kissing the signet ring on the swollen fingers.

"Terrible journey," the bishop announced, "Terrible. But duty is duty."

"Duty?" William glanced back at Maud, she shrugged almost imperceptibly. "What duty would that be, your grace? I'm afraid we did not receive your message."

The man looked at him, narrowing his eyes. "I sent a contingent of men ahead by road, have they not arrived?" he demanded.

William glanced at his closest guard who appeared just as baffled as he felt.

"No, your grace," he shook his head. "They must have been delayed." William furrowed his brow. Who was this man? And why had he so suddenly demanded their hospitality? "Wouldn't you be more comfortable perhaps at the King's house at Clipstone?" he asked, maintaining his half-bow and making use of his most obsequious tone.

"Undoubtedly. But you can accommodate me well enough for a day or so." The bishop squinted up at the shadow of the looming castle, his face protected from the rain by several loyal servants holding an ornate canopy. "Besides," he continued, "this is not merely a social visit." He began a long and weary journey up the cold stone steps to the entrance, pursued by his efficient retinue and curious host. "I am here, not in my capacity as bishop, but as a representative of the king."

"The king!" William couldn't prevent revealing his surprise.

"Yes." The bishop turned back to him, a smile on his full lips. "You hadn't forgotten him already, had you?"

3

SISTER IN NEED

Robyn and Littlejohn wound their way along a familiar deer track. They kept low and quiet though it had been several miles since they had seen any sign of the mysterious soldiers.

High above them, the bright green leaves of summer were already beginning to turn to gold and bronze as the trees whispered in the early evening wind.

Suddenly Littlejohn raised a hand.

Robyn immediately halted and crouched low to the ground listening. There was a faint moaning, the sound of someone or something in pain.

Then a short sharp shout, "Get up dammit!"

Littlejohn turned to Robyn, his eyebrows raised and she returned his look of curious surprise. Without further conversation, the pair of outlaws edged closer to the disturbance.

Staying hidden, Robyn peered through the undergrowth.

A dark grey donkey, carrying several bulging saddle-bags, was sitting on the ground, reclining like a stubborn cat, while a nun, in a white tunic and cowl, with a dark scapular and black veil, pulled uselessly upon his bridle. The large, wooden cross around her neck swung frantically as she muttered obscenities at the disinterested animal.

"Damn you, you useless beast, can you not work in my favour for once in your worthless little life?"

Robyn gasped. She had never heard a nun raise her voice, let alone shout an obscenity. She had to bite down on her lips and squeeze her hand over her mouth lest the laugh that shook her belly escape and reveal their whereabouts.

Littlejohn grinned at her. He clearly felt the same amusement at stumbling upon such an unusual display.

If Robyn hadn't supped on quite so much mead, she might still have paid the woman the respect her position demanded. As it was, when Littlejohn gave a tiny nod toward the nun and Robyn saw the glint of mischief in his eye, she understood his idea at once and agreed furiously. On the silent count of three, the pair of them sprung from the undergrowth.

"Greetings, Sister," Robyn exclaimed, genuflecting with extravagance.

But Robyn was shocked again when the woman pulled a sword from one of the many leather packs and swirled around pointing it directly at her chest. "There's nothing for you here, vagrant," the nun snarled.

Robyn had clearly underestimated the self-sufficiency of the lone woman and instinctively went to draw her bow. But upon remembering it was snapped in two, she raised her hands in surrender. "We mean no harm, Sister."

"We're just two humble foresters, passin'," Littlejohn said, leaning casually upon his stave, despite the woman's drawn weapon. She turned to him, a dark scowl upon her brow. "We thought, didn't we Rob, that we might offer some assistance to a lone sister in need."

"I assure you," the woman spoke without a trace of a Saxon accent, and Robyn suspected she must come from a wealthy Norman family. "I am in need of no assistance, especially not from a pair of ruffians, such as yourselves."

"Ruffians, so we are Rabbit?" Littlejohn cast a twinkling glance at Robyn, who sniggered in response.

"Indeed, we are!" Robyn replied, "Although I know not what we have done to warrant such unusually high praise!" She bowed again at the sister, as Littlejohn guffawed.

"Yes, well you are very droll the pair of you, but I would ask that you leave me to go about my business unharassed."

"So we will." Littlejohn nodded, leaning on his staff unmoving.

"Aye," Robyn agreed, reclining against a tree to appear to the world as if she were nothing but nonchalant, "we'll not stop you leaving." Robyn folded her arms and turned her face to the last rays of the evening sun as if preparing herself for a nap.

The sister muttered angrily but turned her attention back to the stubborn donkey, which only let out a groan of refusal as she pulled upon the beast's bridle.

Littlejohn sniggered, and shook his head but said nothing.

The young sister sighed heavily and threw down the rope. "And you think you can do any better?" she demanded.

Littlejohn looked around as if he couldn't see who spoke. "Who goes there?" he asked, feigning confusion.

Robyn followed his lead and jumped up, feigning shock when she saw the sister, as if noticing her for the first time. "Why 'tis a second nun, Littlejohn! Greetings Sister!" she exclaimed, bowing extravagantly. "Are you searching for your fellow sister? We saw her a while ago, did we not, fellow ruffian?"

"Aye, we did, we did," Littlejohn replied, scratching his beard, "but we cannot tell you which way she went as she was so quick and capable and needed not the help of two ruffians such as us."

"Aye," Robyn added, struggling to hold her voice steady, "She was so quick in fact, 'tis almost as if we did not see her leave at all."

"Neither of you are amusing in the slightest."

Robyn couldn't hold in the laugh any longer, and it burst from her like steam from under the lid of a stewing pot.

Littlejohn chuckled. "We mean no harm by it," he explained, his voice soft and friendly, "but if you need assistance, then what little we have, we can share with a friend who's walked a long way, carrying a heavy burden." He pulled a small crust of bread from one of his many pockets and stepped forward.

To Robyn's surprise, the woman nodded and smiled slightly at this. "Thank you, kind sir, you do the Lord's work." She reached out to accept the offer.

But Littlejohn snapped his hand away from hers. "I were talking to him." He nodded toward the donkey, who at that instant heaved itself from the ground and trotted over to take up Littlejohn's offer.

The sister's face reddened and her eyes widened in what seemed to Robyn something closer to panic than anger. Seeing the young woman's fear ended Robyn's merry game instantly.

"The offer of hospitality extends to you, of course, Sister," she spoke with her gentlest of tones, "Please excuse our merry making, we've had a devil of a day." Robyn winced as she realised her language, but the nun seemed not to notice and was instead fixated on Littlejohn and his easy taming of her charge.

A thick, heavy glob of rain splashed on Robyn's tunic, followed hard by a second against her hood. The sister gasped and tutted as they all realised the torrent that was about to be unleashed upon their heads.

"Will you at least," Robyn had to raise her voice to be heard over the sudden downpour, "will you at least take up our offer of shelter?"

The sister glanced at Robyn, her bright green eyes were remarkably beautiful, and they sparkled like a cat's. Her gaze was so intense, Robyn almost believed the young woman could read her intentions as easily as she might read a book.

With one last glance back at Littlejohn and the easy command he had taken of her donkey. The sister turned to Robyn and gave a curt nod of assent.

"I am at your mercy," she said.

Although there was something about the young woman's manner that made Robyn wonder if perhaps, in truth, it was the other way round.

4

THE LIFE OF A SAINT

Cold meats, boiled eggs, cheeses, bread, wine and ale were brought out plate by plate and jug by jug by the harried and disgruntled servants. They had been summoned from their late evening duties by William's grim-faced and ancient steward, Thomas, and forced to provide a second supper to their lord.

The honoured guest had seated himself in William's own chair at the head of the table and a new fire raged in the large stone hearth behind him using up much of the fuel William had started saving for the winter.

The bishop grumbled intermittently as he ate. "Cold meat? Cold meat? And served to a man of my rank? What kind of a house are you keeping here, Nottingham? You are fortunate that my taste is humble and my needs are few." The red-faced man glugged down another goblet of the best Touraine wine, before patting his face with a clean kerchief and moving on from the discarded bones of a partridge to a freshly cooked veal steak. "Ah, hot veal, that's better Nottingham!" He reached out and slapped the sheriff hard on the back before slicing a too-large morsel of meat and forcing it between his gaping jaws. He clamped down with a groan of satisfaction and held out his goblet for yet more wine.

"Had we been forewarned, your grace," Maud's tone was cordial but William could sense the loathing bubbling within, "we may have better prepared our kitchen to suit your tastes."

The bishop's eyes snapped around, landing on Maud and making no effort to conceal his aversion to her words. "And I am certain that the kitchen would not be the only thing *prepared* for my tastes, eh?"

The insinuation turned William's blood cold. What did the man know? What was the man here to do? Was he insinuating that he knew they were hiding something? Would he discover the promise of silver to Prince John? Did he already know of it and was merely toying with him much as a cat toys with a broken-winged bird? Would William be arrested? Would he be taken from Nottingham and led to the gallows for treason? Would they slice his guts from his body while he screamed?

The thought made him lightheaded. He pushed his trencher away, even the few morsels he had taken for the bishop's sake were too much for him to consider.

Then the bishop turned his attention to William. "Do you allow your wife to talk to all your guests in that way Nottingham? Or is her insolence reserved only for those who serve our king?"

His discomfort must have been clear as his wife came to his rescue immediately. "Of course, we all serve the king, your grace. But you must excuse my temper, we have not long suffered a terrible bereavement."

William knew that Maud did not use the murder of their nephew Theobald lightly, and he was thankful that the bishop turned his attention away from him again. But Maud was not excused from the man's tongue despite the confession of her heartbreak.

"I think, my lady, that you could do with a few lessons in obedience." The bishop pointed at Maud with the sharp end of his knife which he then plunged into a gobbet of veal. He thrust the meat between his jaws as he continued to reprimand her, chewing enthusiastically. "You have heard of Saint Osyth?" He didn't wait for Maud to reply but went on with another chunk of veal pinioned upon his blade and awaiting entry to the endlessly ravenous mouth. "Remarkable woman, St Osyth; she possessed the quality of obedience. As a child, she drowned in a river but so obedient was she, and so loved by the Lord our God in heaven, that when she was found, the Abbess prayed for her restoration," his tone had gone beyond conversation and it was clear he was delivering lines from a well-practised sermon, "the Abbess then commanded Osyth to arise from the river, and obediently, she did as she was bidden and returned with them to the abbey."

"I shall endeavour to follow her example," Maud replied. She turned her eyes to her lap, which had the effect of making her appear demure, although William suspected it was because she could no longer stand to look at the man and it was taking every ounce of strength she possessed to keep from screaming.

"Refused marriage at first you know," the bishop continued, ignoring Maud's obvious discomfort, "said she was married to the church. I've written a book; 'The Life of St Osyth'," he continued blithely, "I ought to give you a copy." He clicked his fingers and immediately, a loyal servant dressed in a long robe of gilded velvet that roused considerable envy in William, stepped forward from the shadows clutching a small chest which he lay upon the table next to the bishop. The bishop pulled a key from a chain on his neck and, upon opening the chest, revealed not a pile of silver, as would normally be held in such a strong box, but something even more precious: two identical books. Each was about the size of his hand and bound in leather with a delicate cross hatch pattern embossed on the front. When the bishop removed one of the thin little volumes, he revealed another exact copy underneath and William suspected the entire box was stacked high with impeccable handcrafted copies.

The bishop handed the book to William who knew it must have taken weeks to craft. One or maybe two of these books could buy him a fairly decent warhorse. "Thank you," William managed to stammer, already planning how he might find a buyer for it.

"Perhaps your husband would be kind enough to read some passages to you?"

"My husband?" Maud asked stiffly, her eyes growing wider as her brow drew lower.

"You don't read Latin yourself, do you?" It was an innocent question but William was all too aware of the dangerous implications of a wrong answer.

William could see, even upon her fixed countenance, that Maud was viciously torn between proving him wrong and keeping one of the most dangerous men in the country on her side. "No," she lied, closing her eyes briefly as if drawing upon her last reserves of serenity. "It would be unseemly for me to read at all, let alone read Latin." She smiled graciously and William was almost convinced of her humility.

"Good, good," the man blustered on, "You don't want a wife that reads, Nottingham, especially not a wife that reads Latin. That is a path that can lead only to misery and sin."

"Of course, your grace," William replied as if it was the most important piece of marriage advice he had ever received.

"You would have been a good candidate for a nunnery," the bishop continued, and it seemed he hadn't given up on kicking the hornet's nest that was Maud's patience. "There's still time, of course," he lifted his goblet to his lips nonchalantly.

Maud and William exchanged a desperate look of impatience. "I am married, your grace." Maud managed.

"Yes, yes," he shook his head as if pondering the obstacle that was Maud and William's marriage. "If only more women such as yourself followed the example of St Osyth and took to the church."

William opened his mouth to speak, desperate to change the subject, but Maud, her knuckles bone-white against the dark burgundy of her gown got there first.

"Your grace," she spoke softly and there was the suggestion of a smirk at her lips, "if more women followed St Osyth's example and joined the church rather than marry, then I fear there may be fewer children to swell the numbers of your flock." She sipped her wine, disguising the smile that dimpled her cheeks, and William was forced to swallow a grin of his own.

"You don't have any children, do you?" If the bishop had killed them both there and then, the silence that followed could not have been more deathly.

It was a long cold minute before William could stammer his response. "N-no, your grace."

Maud stood suddenly, grazing the heavy wooden chair against the flagstones. "It is late," she said and her words sounded as though they were taking the last breath in her body to utter. "I should leave you, gentlemen, to talk." She turned and stalked from the room, her skirts trailing behind her and William had to fight the urge to rush after her.

If he had been a more powerful man, William thought, he may well have murdered the bishop for his slight. As it was, he was weak and had to make do with gripping the arm of his chair and raising his glass of wine. "To your good health, your grace."

"Read much Latin do you, Nottingham?"

"Not as much as your learned self, sire, I'm sure."

"Language of God you know, language of God," he trailed off.

William resisted the urge to point out that if the 'humble' bishop was capable of writing in two languages then the all-knowing-God was surely capable of using more than one. "Fine weather we're having for the time of year is it not?" asked William in a desperate attempt to fill the void of silence left by Maud.

"Don't try to avoid the subject, Nottingham!" The bishop turned on him, with pink cheeks and wine-stained lips.

William stared, dumbfounded for a moment. "L-Latin?" he asked.

"Treason!" barked the bishop, banging the table.

"Treason, your grace?" William felt sick. He could feel his last sip of wine tugging at his throat to come back up, the floor seemed to sway beneath his chair like the deck of a ship at sea, and it was all he could do to grip the arms to stop himself crumbling into a heap on the ground before his accuser.

"Yes," the bishop furrowed his brow, "You charged some lowly baron's wife? Leaming? Foxton? Oxley?"

"Loxley!" William cried, the twisting guilt falling from him in an instant, "The Baroness of Loxley," he smiled sighing with relief as he did so.

"Loxley! That's the one!" The bishop barked in triumph and his wine swished over the edge of his goblet. "So, it's true."

"Yes," William nodded and feigned solemnity, "I'm afraid so, your grace, just last month-"

"Treason is a matter for the king."

"Well, yes, of course, and I intended to wait for King Richard's return-"

"And yet you did not notify Chancellor Longchamp?"

William's mouth hung open for a moment. "Well, as you say," he was getting uncomfortably hot, he pulled at the collar of his tunic, "treason is a matter for the king-" he stammered.

"And Chancellor Longchamp is the king's justice!" The silverware clattered as he banged the table again. "Therefore, if it is a matter for the king, then it is a matter for Longchamp, and if it is a matter for Longchamp," he peered at William with dewy blue eyes, reddened with drink, "then it is a matter for me."

"Hereford!" William whispered his realisation, the man was the Bishop of Hereford, a man of the cloth but nevertheless a man of government. King Richard's government. He ought to have recognised the banner, known the livery by sight, but it was too late now. The man was here, supping his wine, partaking of his bread... and if so much as a breath of their promise of a thousand silver to aid in Prince John's campaign reached his ears then they would all be condemned. Not only sentenced to death but tortured until he or his wife revealed the name of every co-conspirator in England and beyond. "Well, I-" he stammered.

"I should like to see the baroness for myself."

"Ah, well-"

"Do you defy me, Nottingham?" His cheeks reddened further as spittle launched from his lips in his rage.

"Well, you see, I had her taken to York-" William winced, knowing the mention of John's most loyal stronghold would surely be enough to confirm the bishop's suspicions.

"York? York? Why York, boy?"

William hadn't been called 'boy' in nearly thirty years. "Well-I...I..."

"They're loyal to the prince, are they not?"

"Yes, but-"

"Prince John may be Lord of Nottinghamshire, boy, but Richard is your king. It is your king to whom you owe your loyalty, and your taxes," he narrowed his eyes at William, "even if your lord and prince may think otherwise."

"Well, yes of course, but you see-" The bishop knew. Or did he know? Did the bishop know of the plans of the prince or did he merely suspect?

"Even Christ was tempted," the bishop warned, ominously, "England is in the desert. We are lost without our king. Lost like Christ in the wilderness and we, like Christ, shall face many temptations, but, like Christ, we must resist. Do you understand Nottingham?"

It was suspicion; suspicions only. But dangerously accurate suspicions. "I think so, but-"

"We must stay loyal to our God and our God-Chosen-King. Much like St Osyth who demonstrated her loyalty to God throughout her life. Incidentally, would you care for a copy of my book?" All threat had gone from his manner as he gestured again for his aid who dutifully brought forth the little chest. But William mutely held up Maud's copy feeling as though every nerve in his body had been shattered.

"Oh, you have one, good, good, now, where was I? Yes, yes, this Baroness Loxley. I expect you to bring her to me first thing in the morning, Nottingham."

"Well, I, -"

"No excuses, man."

"She's gone," he finally spat the words and was so relieved to have explained that he had overlooked the torrent of rage that would inevitably follow his admission.

"Gone?" stammered the bishop, "Gone?" The man looked perilously close to bursting.

"Escaped, your grace," William replied breathlessly, feeling as though his body had shrunk in on itself and crumpled his courage to nothing.

"Escaped? When? How? How could you let a thing like this happen, man?" He banged his goblet on the table, splashing red wine on the abandoned remnants of his veal. "You wouldn't have had a thing like this happening in De Lacy's time!"

That's because, William thought, *Sheriff De Lacy had triple the men and double the income. Both of which he has taken with him on crusade*. Although all he could say out loud was, "No, your grace."

"Well, no matter," the Bishop of Hereford growled his words, but the worst of the anger appeared to have left him, "But I expect in the future, that you call on me when you have matters for the king's justice."

"Yes, your grace," William sat up, tentatively. Was that it? Was that the entirety of the reprimand? He tried not to let the relief swallow him.

"Good. Now that we've cleared that up-" the bishop interrupted himself to pat his chest and then belch loudly at the ceiling, "bad wine always has that effect." He leaned closer to William, conspiratorially. "There is something I need you to do for me. Now ordinarily I would expect the use of the king's foresters, but since they have all..."

"Left?" William finished.

"Gone to risk their lives in the Holy Land in the name of Jesus Christ our Lord and Saviour," he made the sign of the cross with his free hand and William quickly followed suit, terrified of falling foul of the man's wrath twice in one conversation.

"Of course, sire," he replied sheepishly.

"I need you to find someone for me."

"Find someone?"

"A vicious, ungodly criminal, who has made a mockery of the Church and runs amuck as if the Devil himself stalked the land."

"A killer?"

"Worse," the bishop replied, his face darkening, "a woman."

5

HOUSEGUEST

Sister Mary stared over their camp. "This is it?" she asked, turning to Robyn. "I had assumed there would be a hovel at least."

Robyn regarded their woodland home. Within a small clearing of hard earth surrounded by shrubs and trees on all sides, were two lean-tos. The frames were of good, strong branches and a slanted wall of skins offered shelter from the current downpour as well as the biting wind that occasionally howled through this part of Sherwood. One was big enough for the great bulk of Littlejohn to rest comfortably, the other was her own. Carpeted with soft furs and surrounded by a few belongings including a green cloak, an extra pair of boots and a couple of empty water skins.

They'd dug a good hearth and had plenty of firewood stacked and ready, kept dry under some skins. They even had a good food store of pheasant and rabbit hanging from a beam across two trees, complemented with a barrel of Merek's (second) finest ale and a small crate of donations including a bunch of thin-looking carrots and a generous block of goat's cheese.

Robyn had moved up in the world since her first night in the woods; half of which had been spent in the branches of a tree and the other on the cold hard ground with not a scrap of blanket to keep out the wind. But even this latest home was nothing compared to the luxury and wealth of Loxley Manor, where the beds were soft, the fires roared, and the shutters kept out the roaring storms. But she didn't know when she would be able to call that place home again.

"There's a fine ditch a mile yonder if you'd rather," Littlejohn muttered. He pushed past, still leading the donkey and went to unpack the beast's heavy cargo.

But Sister Mary leapt forward, pushing him aside. "It will do for one night," she slapped him away from her luggage, "but please, let me."

Littlejohn shrugged and left her to struggle, turning his attention to stacking some wood and setting the fire as best he could in the rain, while Robyn shook her head marvelling at her own patience as she offered her services to the woman of the cloth. "Allow me," she said, holding out her hands to help.

Sister Mary had unhooked a heavy, leather saddlebag and was looking about clutching it. "Is there..." Sister Mary began, "is there somewhere safe to keep this?"

"Aye," Robyn answered casually, "I'll hide it with the—"

Littlejohn coughed suddenly and Robyn caught herself from revealing their treasure trove, but not quite in time. Sister Mary narrowed her eyes and glanced from one to the other. "Hide it with what?" she asked slowly.

"It will be safe down here," Robyn said quickly, taking the bag from Sister Mary's arms. It was heavier than she had expected. She let out a grunt as she placed it next to their barrel of ale and pretended that was where she had intended all along.

"It needs to be particularly safe," Sister Mary pushed.

"Aye," Littlejohn agreed, his fire was starting to crackle and grow, Robyn was surprised how thankful she was for the promise of heat, the nights were already starting to draw in. "We'll keep an eye on it for you."

"It's just," there was an air of something Robyn couldn't quite place in the nun's tone, "it is an awful lot of money."

Littlejohn stood up straight, eyebrows raised. Robyn stared. Why was this unaccompanied nun carrying 'an awful lot of money' through an unfamiliar wood on the back of a reluctant donkey?

"For the orphans." Sister Mary looked down, as if ashamed of having admitted her secret. When the sister's dark green eyes locked with hers, Robyn felt a sudden pang and was certain that under those heavy God-laden robes was a young woman of remarkable beauty.

"Orphans?" Robyn asked. It seemed to her that whatever mission this young woman was on, it was either highly secret, highly dangerous or both. Yet, here she was embarking upon it alone. Now that Sister Mary had entrusted her secret to Robyn, it was surely her duty to help the sister see it through?

"What orphans?" Littlejohn barked, breaking Robyn's trance.

Sister Mary raised her chin and Robyn was suddenly reminded of a defiant look that Marian would so often throw her way and the memory bit at her. She had not felt whole since she'd last seen Marian and that had been far too long ago.

"Orphans of the crusade," Sister Mary replied.

Littlejohn didn't appear convinced but Robyn's heart gave a leap. Had the Crusade lost so many already? Did the sister have news of the dead? Was Robyn's own father among them? She opened her mouth to ask but Littlejohn interjected.

"Oh aye?" he said, "Well, there can't be many, it's only been goin' six-month."

Those same dark green eyes narrowed once again. "And yet, those few that there are, need our help. And I think they would prefer it if the money raised for their aid was not squandered through our ineptitude." Sister Mary had a way of saying 'our' that made Robyn absolutely certain she meant 'your'.

Robyn smiled. She liked the spirit of anyone able to stand up to the brute strength of Littlejohn with that much defiance.

"It's alright," Robyn said, stepping between the pair by way of becoming a peacemaker, "I'll put it somewhere safer." Robyn heaved the bags from the ground and stopped Littlejohn from contesting with a grin and a rueful shake of the head. "For the orphans," she said and hoped she wasn't one of them.

He rolled his eyes but didn't protest, and Robyn pushed her way through the dense foliage and ripe, red berries of a wayfaring-tree. She knelt, resting the heavy bag on the earth with a thud that jangled its contents, then felt around in the dirt for the edge of a cloth concealed by loose earth. Rolling back a tanned hide that was adorned with enough foliage to deceive even the closest scrutiny, Robyn revealed a hole roughly three feet across and nearly two feet deep. At the bottom of, what she had guessed must be a caved-in badger set, was a fine chest with a shining new lock, the key to which hung on twine around Robyn's neck. Hidden inside the chest was a small fortune in silver, formerly the property of one High Sheriff of Nottinghamshire and Derbyshire. Robyn grinned at the memory.

Her intention had been only to rescue her mother, sister and brothers from the clutches of the sheriff, but in doing so she had inadvertently liberated a thousand pieces of silver. Most of it had now been used to pay the quarterly rents for the poorest tenants of Nottingham and the surrounding villages. But a good portion, nigh on three hundred silver, enough for two full suits of armour and a brace of warhorses to match, was still waiting to be put to good use.

Robyn rolled the new bag into the hideaway and heard the heavy clink of coins as it turned and thudded into the hole. The bag wasn't as big as her own chest, but the weight alone told her there must be double the silver at least. There would certainly be enough to feed a few orphans for a while.

When she returned to the clearing, she found the air thick and the silence excruciating. Sister Mary was releasing the donkey from the last of its prison of pouches, bags and blankets, while Littlejohn was crouching in front of the fire roasting chunks of pheasant skewered on a sharpened stick.

"That's me done," Littlejohn said suddenly; he stood and slid the first piece of meat off the skewer with his teeth before grabbing his stave, nodding to Robyn, and disappearing through the foliage.

"Your husband seems... nice," Sister Mary said, without looking up from the last buckle.

"He's not my husband," Robyn quickly corrected, shocked at even the hint of such an idea. Sister Mary turned to her with eyebrows raised. "No," Robyn said quickly, "We're not—we're nothing—we're friends. That's that."

"As you prefer," the sister replied with a shrug.

Robyn didn't like the knowing tone the sister used, especially when she was so clearly wrong. She had half a mind to shock the nun by telling her about Marian, but she stopped herself. For one thing, she was unsure exactly how to describe Marian. She hesitated to even think the word 'sweethearts'; the thought made her gut wobble and her chest hot. They were friends, wonderful friends, they had known each other forever, adored one another for years... and then that kiss... when the whole world held its breath and she had felt, from her toes to her nose-tip... complete.

"Are you going to cook me dinner or not?" Sister Mary stood with her hands on her hips and snapped Robyn abruptly back to reality.

The sudden urge to grab her bow and wander off after Littlejohn overwhelmed her. But the sister was a woman of God and if her father had taught her anything, it was that you should never get on the wrong side of God, no matter how rude his representatives on earth may be. Besides, she remembered, her bow was snapped in two.

"Of course," Robyn answered with a smile more forced than it had been all evening. She diced up a few morsels of pheasant on the stump of a tree and imitated Littlejohn's method of roasting them on a sharpened stick. As she crouched down beside the fire, thick drops of rain sizzled and spat in the flames. She pulled her hood as far as she could over her head and hugged herself with her free hand.

"Do you have any bread to go with that meat?" Sister Mary asked.

Robyn turned to her and stared as the rain thickened and the fire sizzled.

"No," she said, finally feeling her patience snapping, "and with all the coin I've just heaved into safekeeping, I've a good mind to make you pay for the pheasant and heavily at that."

"You wouldn't!" the sister replied, aghast.

"Don't tempt me," Robyn muttered, thinking it wasn't actually such a bad idea.

6

NO GOOD DEED

Robyn awoke as the rays of sunlight finally pressed too hard on her eyes to resist the day.

She rolled onto her back, craving a breakfast that was anything other than roasted meat. The fire had died in the night, but the embers were still warm, and it wouldn't take her long to get it going again. Perhaps, when she went to the river she could catch a perch or a carp. That would at least be a change of flavour.

She sat up, reaching for her bow and groaned as she remembered once again that it was broken. How many times would she forget? And yet, she groaned each time afresh. The pain of remembering seemed never to weaken.

Littlejohn's nest of furs was empty. Although Robyn had been sure that she'd heard him returning from his overnight hunt not more than an hour or so ago.

She looked around and was surprised that their dinner guest was nowhere to be seen. Robyn's first thought was that Sister Mary had gone somewhere private for morning prayers. But immediately she dismissed that notion; the donkey was gone too.

She sprang up, then halted. *Why was she uneasy? The woman had asked for shelter, they had provided it. Why shouldn't Sister Mary move on once she'd had her rest?* No doubt a nun was used to rising before dawn, so naturally, she would have already left. And it must have been Sister Mary moving around so quietly about the camp that had made Robyn so sure that Littlejohn had returned.

There was nothing strange about it.

She breathed slowly, shaking off her sudden start and decided now was as good a time as any to head down to the river.

The cold, fresh water ran along the forest floor just a few yards away, down a steep incline. It was knee-deep at this stretch of the river, and too far to cross in a leap, but it gave Littlejohn and Robyn a place to wash, drink and, if they were lucky, catch a few fish.

She threw off her boots and carried out her morning ablutions. The water made her gasp, but it was enough to wake her and her mind began to wander.

Why had Sister Mary been so quiet? It didn't seem like her to leave Robyn undisturbed. It would have been more like her to wake Robyn and demand breakfast. She should be delighted that the woman had gone. She had been spared a morning of disdainful nagging. And yet...

Was she disappointed that Sister Mary had left without saying goodbye? Surely, she hadn't expected gratitude from someone who was so obviously incapable of it? But there was a spark about that woman that Robyn had liked... and those green eyes of hers had the power to make her heart stop even when they were no more than a memory.

Did she miss the companionship of Marian so much that the company of even a foul-tempered nun was welcomed and then mourned?

But then, as Robyn splashed the ice-cold water on her face, the thought struck her in an instant. *The money!*

She turned and ran, leaving her boots by the riverbank. Sister Mary wouldn't have known where her money had been hidden. She'd have to wake Robyn to fetch it. Had Sister Mary seen where Robyn buried it? No, she couldn't have. Not without Littlejohn noticing.

Had she kept a note of where she'd seen Robyn disappear to, returning later to search for it in the dead of night?

Possibly.

But why?

She could have just woken Robyn and demanded she fetch it. It wasn't out of politeness that she let Robyn sleep; she was sure of that. It wasn't her demure personality that had kept Sister Mary from demanding her aid.

Robyn charged into the camp. Fear swirling in her gut.

Surely, she was wrong?

Sister Mary was a woman of the cloth.

She leapt over the warm embers of the hearth, brushed through the branches of the wayfarer-tree, and slammed onto her knees with a hard thud.

She clawed around in the dirt, yanking off the hide as soon as she found the edge.

But she sighed. Then grinned as relief swept through her.

The saddlebags were gone, but the chest was still there. She laughed and shook her head. How could she have even considered the idea?

She went to replace the hide covering but hesitated, staring at the chest. It nagged her. It was just a feeling. Just a wild thought.

The lock was intact.

She was wrong. She had to be wrong. She should never have suspected a nun of ever touching her silver.

And yet... Robyn's hand would not allow her to replace the covering. The chest would not let her walk away.

It didn't matter. God couldn't hold it against her for checking.

There was an awful lot that God could hold against her but being suspicious of a woman of the cloth was nothing. It wasn't as if she was openly accusing anyone. It wasn't as though she was preparing the branding iron.

Tired of her own suspicions, Robyn snapped. If it would quieten her mind then she would look.

She grabbed the key and pulled the cord over her neck, talking herself out of checking even as she slid the key in the lock and threw back the lid.

Robyn gasped.

A hand went to her mouth and then straight to her stomach as a sickness threatened her twisting gut. She cried out, voicing something between a yelp of pain and a scream of rage.

Her chest, her precious chest that only yesterday had been brimming with enough silver to feed a hundred men at a king's banquet, was empty.

Sister Mary was a thief.

7

MASTER THIEF

Robyn didn't have to look far for the deep tracks of the laden donkey, and she didn't have to follow the tracks for more than a mile before she could follow the sound of swearing.

Sure enough, on a road thick with churned mud, she found Sister Mary once again venting her fury at her unwilling cohort.

"You need a more faithful accomplice," Robyn said, clutching the stitch in her side and wishing she'd taken a moment to put on her boots.

But rather than laugh or admit defeat, the sister drew her sword once more.

"Come even one step closer, and I shall run you through!" she shouted, "Don't think for a moment that I won't."

Robyn's hand almost went to reach for her bow, but of course, it was laying on the ground back at the camp, snapped in two. Instead, the only weapon she could draw was her knife. She held her hands up, less in defeat and more in an attempt to show that she meant no harm.

"Please," she urged, "I merely request you return our silver. We are not common thieves, some people are relying on that coin, they need that money. You wouldn't see a child starve to death, would you?"

"I couldn't give two shits about your bastard children," the sister snarled.

Robyn nodded. "I had a feeling you weren't a real nun."

"Actually," to Robyn's surprise, the woman smiled, "I am. And if you don't mind, I shall be on my way." She pulled on the reins of the donkey, but it was no good.

Robyn laughed. "You can leave him with me, I'll take the silver for his upkeep and we shall call it even."

"I am in no mind for your tiresome japes," there was agony in her frustrated cry and Robyn almost felt pity for her; whatever her situation was, it was obviously desperate.

Robyn stepped forward; her bare feet were numb with cold in the wet mud. "I mean no harm," she spoke calmly, reassuring the raging woman, "perhaps I can help you."

Robyn reached for the bridle but leapt back as the sister's sword cut through the air.

"Go," Sister Mary cried, lashing left and right with the sword as Robyn stumbled backward through the mud, "Go or I shall run you through!"

But Robyn wasn't about to give up, not with this woman taking the hope of so many people of Nottingham. As Sister Mary dropped her guard, Robyn leapt forward. But the woman was swift. The sister turned on her heel and sliced, cutting the cloth of Robyn's tunic as she leapt back to avoid the blade.

Robyn slipped, landing hard in the thick mud and looked up to see the tip of the blade at her throat. "If I had my bow-" Robyn snarled through gritted teeth.

"You still wouldn't stand a chance."

"Aye Lassie, we're all mightily impressed with your skill."

Sister Mary spun around to see Littlejohn, stave in hand, standing between her and her treasure-laden donkey.

In a flash, she turned upon him, her feet light, her sword twirling, she leapt. But Littlejohn was quicker still. With a hard crack, he smashed the sword from her hand and it went soaring up into the air. Robyn leapt to her feet and caught it with one hand as it flew back down to earth.

With the giant of a man on one side and a muddy, sword-wielding outlaw on the other, Sister Mary looked about to turn and flee.

"Don't test us, Lassie," Littlejohn said, his voice gruff with lack of sleep. Robyn was glad that he had clearly distrusted the woman enough to stay close by and awake all night patrolling their camp.

"What do you intend to do with me?" Sister Mary asked, looking from one to the other, and Robyn was delighted to hear a note of fear crack the thief's cocky tone.

"Oh," Robyn answered, glancing at Littlejohn with a grin, "only what you deserve.

GOLD.

Robyn didn't know how much, but it was a beautiful sight; buttery, pure and so bright in the sun that it seemed as though the light was emanating directly from it. Her mouth dropped open as she reached inside the bag and caressed the golden discs. They weren't English, she picked one up and inspected the Latin inscription, a cross embossed in the centre, not unlike the heavy golden altar cross buried amongst the coins and pearl prayer beads. Robyn didn't have to think too hard to guess that the gold was stolen from a church, and not a country parish, but a great abbey, perhaps even a cathedral.

Littlejohn stood over her and sucked in the air between his teeth as he stared. Then he passed her a leather pouch around the size of a quiver. "Found this in one o' them bags."

Robyn rolled open the pouch to discover a confusing collection of bizarre, metal implements.

"Those are for a surgeon, I'm taking them to him," Sister Mary called over. Her tone had lost its fear and growing irritation was returning to her voice. They'd strung her up, Robyn had bound her wrists then Littlejohn had slung the rope over a branch, pulling it just tight enough to force the thief onto her toes. Then he'd secured it to the tree trunk, giving them a chance to investigate exactly what the poor donkey had been refusing to carry.

"Oh aye?" asked Littlejohn, turning to the nun with his thick, bushy eyebrows raised, "and is the surgeon a scafflocke same as thee?"

"How dare you?" In her anger she pulled at the rope, pirouetting as she did so.

"Scafflocke?" Robyn asked, none the wiser.

"Aye," Littlejohn nodded gravely, his voice a low growl, "these are the tools of a lock breaker, a scaffer, this one ain't some petty cutpurse Robyn, we've found ourselves a master thief." He glanced back at the young woman as she fought the rope binding her hands. "Thing is, what do we do with her?"

"Listen," Sister Mary called over, "you've had your amusement, why not cut me down, and we can all be on our way?"

"I'll cut you down alright!" Littlejohn turned to their

prisoner, fury on his lips, but Robyn sprang up, placing a hand upon his arm.

"Hold back Giant, she has a fair suggestion."

"That thief was not more than one inch away from running you through, Rabbit."

He was right, Robyn had been certain, in that moment, that the woman wouldn't hesitate to strike, and yet Robyn couldn't find any anger within her. In Sister Mary she saw too much of herself; a thief, alone, on the run, frightened. If she could not forgive this woman then what forgiveness could she ever expect for herself? She opened her mouth to speak but at that moment the donkey arose startled and hurried off back toward camp. Immediately, Robyn could hear the reason behind it; heavy hooves.

"What are you doing?" Sister Mary demanded as, between them, Robyn and Littlejohn hurried to grab the gold and saddlebags before scuttling off into the undergrowth to hide them.

Sister Mary shouted obscenities and, after heaving the gold-filled bag to the ground with a jangling thud, Robyn turned to release their prisoner, her knife ready to cut the rope. But Littlejohn grabbed her shoulder, pointing.

It was too late.

Four horsemen, decked out in the familiar red with a green cross and crowns of Nottingham, took only a moment to surround Sister Mary. Robyn and Littlejohn ducked down in the bushes, listening to the scraps of taunts the guards reeled off.

"We should never have left the poor lass," Littlejohn was pale and his brows furrowed.

"You were ready to hand her over a moment ago."

"Aye," he shook his head, "But them blackguards know not true justice."

"She's a scafflocke, surely she can just break out of that old castle gaol?"

"Not without the tools of the trade, Rabbit."

Robyn took a deep breath as she watched the guards jeer at their prisoner then cut her down and lead her away. "Then I shall have to get her tools to her," Robyn said.

Littlejohn looked at her for a long moment, then shook his head. "You can't just walk into Nottingham castle."

"Maybe not," Robyn replied, picking at a scrap of sheep's wool caught on a thorn, "but I think I know someone who can."

8

OLD NORA

The woman carried a basket laden with bread, cheese and clay bottles of drink. Although heavy, she managed it well with her bent legs and hunched back. Her face was bandaged with old, dirty rags. Spots of discolouration hinted at sores or wounds hidden beneath and what little of her flesh did show was dark with dirt. Her hair, white and wispy as wool, poked out from her cowl, and she leaned heavily on a rough, mud speckled stick that appeared as though it had been plucked from a ditch that morning.

The lone guard on the gates of Nottingham Castle paid her no heed as she hobbled through and made her way across the inner ballium toward the castle gaol. She paused a moment watching the strange new men-at-arms, decked out in a livery of gold and red quartered with a white star, as they went about their training. One glanced her way, a man she would call young, but for his fine, white beard. Then the woman turned and hobbled off in the direction of the small castle gaol.

The young lad on duty, with a wisp of a half-hearted

moustache, stood upright and alert as she wandered in through the stone arch.

"Who goes there?" he shouted, a strain of panic in his tone as he fumbled to ready his pike.

The woman looked around with her single exposed eye, searching the barely lit guardroom before landing on him.

"Good day to you!" she announced, her voice was cracked and broken, "Come 'ere laddie." A gnarled hand, gloved in the same dirty rags, emerged from the folds of her robes and a single finger beckoned the young lad. "Let old Nora take a good look at you." Nervously the young man took a step forward, trying not to show his distaste. "Oh, it's Martha's lad, ain't it? Oh, whatsit… Bert?" He nodded at her, his mouth agape. "Ah, your ma's a good lass, so she is. Up every week t'Alms House. Not seen you since you were so high."

"Aye, well…" he fumbled for a moment, "I work long days 'ere, like."

"That you do lad, that you do." The old woman patted his chest and went to move off toward the gaol. "You's a good lad."

"Ay-up!" he called after her, and the old woman halted, "you're not to go down there, that's the castle gaol that is."

"Aye, laddie, that's why I'm here, I'm bringing food for prisoners," she chuckled slightly and shook her head.

"Nay, I were told they's not to have nuthin'."

"Of course not, young laddie, you give 'em nuthin' 'cause old Nora's here, ain't that right?" she chuckled again.

The lad's hands twisted on the handle of his pike as his weight shifted from one foot to the other. "I dunno." He looked back along the corridor as if hoping another guard would appear to offer their support.

"Oh, I almost forgot meself." The old woman shuffled

over to a little wooden table and three-legged stool pushed into a corner. She heaved out a clay bottle and landed it with a thud on the tabletop. "That's good cider that is, but don't be telling none of t'other lads, or they'll all be wantin' some of old Nora's treats!" She chuckled again and turned, shuffling off down the dark stairs into the gaol. The young lad, Bert, looked from her to the cider, then shook his head with a sigh and returned to his post.

"Alms, alms for the prisoner!" the old woman called out as she shuffled along, peering in each cell as she passed. In the third one along, she saw a young man, unkempt and crouched on the floor, his head in his hands. She paused, uncertain, then pulled a loaf from her basket and pushed it through the bars, hissing. The young man looked up at her, startled. "Take it," she said, waving it about. "Go on."

He was confused for a moment and then leapt forward, grabbing the bread and devouring it without thanks. Under her heavy bandages, the stranger smiled at his unspoken gratitude then moved on. She peered into each empty cell before finally landing on the prisoner she had been searching for.

Balled up on the thin, wooden bench, with her back to the bars, was a young woman. She wore a nun's habit but her black hair fell loose.

"Alms for the prisoner," the old woman called out.

"Go away!" the nun replied.

But the stranger with the basket chuckled, then spoke in a lower but far more youthful voice, "Oh, I think you'll want these alms."

The young woman sprang up, turning to look at the stranger, startled. "You!" she stammered.

"Robyn Hood, at your service," Robyn replied. She shed

the gait of the old woman and bowed extravagantly just as she had done when she had first met the sister in the woods.

"Come to scorn, have you? Come to laugh at the prisoner?" Sister Mary spoke with bitterness. She remained seated at the bench in the dark rather than stepping forward into the weak lantern light.

"No," Robyn corrected, "I've come to your rescue."

"Rescue! How dare you! You put me here!"

Robyn laughed. "It was no more than you deserve, you are a thief after all."

"I'm not the only thief between the pair of us!"

Robyn chuckled with a shake of her head. "I'll be off then shall I?" she asked, turning from the cell, but Sister Mary rushed to the bars.

"No! No, don't leave, don't leave." She sighed heavily. With her hands together under her scapular, and her head low and pressed against the bars, Robyn believed she could almost have been a repentant nun. "What's your plan?" Her voice was quieter, calmer and convincingly submissive.

Robyn grinned. She pulled the young nun's sword from under her many layers of tattered rags, set it aside and then rummaged for a package at the bottom of her basket, opening it to reveal the sister's set of lock picks. "This," she announced triumphantly.

"That's it, is it?" Sister Mary snarled, "That's your plan?"

"Well," said Robyn, affronted and slightly confused, "if you managed the lock on that chest, you can manage the locks on these old things." Robyn shook the rusting bars of the cage. "Wait until nightfall, then make a run for it. There'll only be one or two guards on duty these days, and they will likely be asleep."

"Just go," Sister Mary's voice was weak and defeated,

she turned from the bars and headed back to the bench in the dark.

Robyn wasn't sure what game she was playing or even if there was a game at all. "Don't you want your things?" Robyn held the handle of the sword and the lockpicks through the bars of the cell, but Sister Mary merely shook her head. No longer even an inch of the sassy wilful spirit Robyn had met the day before in Sherwood. "What's going on? Just take them, this is no jest, I came to help."

"But I can't use them, Robyn." Sister Mary looked at her with red eyes. There was a crack in her voice.

Robyn knew there must be something terribly wrong. "What? Why?" she asked, her voice gentle but firm, "Why can't you use them?"

Sister Mary bit her lip and her jaw twitched as though she were holding back a torrent, but instead of voicing an answer, she stepped forward. She lifted her hands from under the scapular and pushed them through the bars.

In the weak lamplight of the gaol, Robyn released a sharp breath and her stomach knotted into a ball of shock and shame.

The rough bandages carelessly thrown around Sister Mary's hands could not hide the dark red blood congealing on her palms and the blistering wounds that had torn the flesh from her fingers. She could barely open her fists and Robyn could clearly see the lines of agony painted on the young woman's features.

"What did they do to you?" Robyn hissed.

9

ORDEAL

Sister Mary sniffed, pulling her hands back into the folds of her clothes. "It was my trial," she was struggling to swallow her sobs, "trial by ordeal."

"So... if those wounds don't heal?"

"In three days, I shall be hanged."

"Hanged?" Robyn gasped, "But-but I thought- I mean- that's not canon law!"

"The Bishop of Hereford works for the king's justice. It's his choice whether he uses church law or the king's law," the sister allowed her voice to crack, "so, thank you for bringing me my things, but I may as well already be dead."

"No," Robyn snarled letting her rage drown out her guilt, "I'm getting you out."

"Out? And how exactly do you expect to do that? Are you a scafflocke now?"

"No. But you are," Robyn said firmly, "and you shall teach me." She placed down the basket and pulled out one of the strange metal implements from the pack. It was a long tool with a ring at one end and an L-shaped bend at the other.

"But the guard, Robyn, he could come to check on you at any moment."

"Then we'll have to work fast." She slid the L-shaped end into the lock on the cell and began poking around aimlessly.

Sister Mary looked beyond Robyn toward the stairs at the end of the corridor. A shadow of fear passed across her features but was gone in an instant. Her face hardened as she looked at Robyn. "You'll need the second one of those."

Robyn nodded and searched through the pack.

"That one," Sister Mary said as Robyn pulled out a similar implement, only this one had a further bend. "Right," she continued, taking a deep breath, "all you have to do is lift the lever with that second one and hold it in place while you throw the ball with the other."

"Sounds simple enough," Robyn said, not knowing what Sister Mary was talking about but hoping she would be able to work it out.

"It is," Sister Mary said firmly, "these locks are nothing compared to the ones at the Priory, even you might be able to do it."

But it wasn't simple.

Lifting the lever would be easy if she could find the lever, but without knowing what she was looking for it was damned near impossible. The pair were muttering obscenities at one another within minutes and under her absurd disguise, sweat was running down Robyn's forehead and into her eyes, only one of which she could see with.

But then with a click, the tool clamped against something and, as she turned it, she felt something give; she was lifting the lever. "I've got it!" she cried.

"Shh!"

Robyn froze.

"He's coming," Sister Mary hissed.

If she moved now the lever would fall. She didn't know how long it would take her to manage that trick again or *if* she would ever be able to manage it. The sweat was trickling down her back and the weight of her outfit was bearing down upon her.

"Nora?" the young guard called across the dark corridor, "you's been a might too long down here, now."

"Just-" Robyn started, panic swelling within her, she found Nora's voice. Crunching her throat into a harsh, gnarled, but cheery voice, "Just give ol' Nora and the sister a moment more, laddie."

But he was edging toward them, she could hear his boots against the stone floor and see the panic in Sister Mary's eyes.

"Hail Mary, full of grace," the nun started, she lay her forehead against the bars, "The Lord is with thee."

This was no time for praying!

The guard was upon them, Robyn had to let go of the lever, she would have to go, she would have to come back later, work out some other gaolbreak. But that would mean leaving the sister to die.

Sister Mary pushed her bloodied hands through the bars, placing them over Robyn's and hiding the half-picked lock. "Holy Mary, Mother of God," she continued in a low mutter, "pray for us sinners, now and at the hour of our death. Amen."

"Right, then Nora-"

"Hail Mary, full of grace," Sister Mary started again, firmer this time, louder. Robyn could think of nothing else to do, so joined her.

"The Lord is with thee," they said together.

"Aye, well." Bert dithered, placing his weight on one foot then the other.

"Blessed art thou among women," they continued, with Sister Mary firmly ignoring the young man, but Robyn turned to look at him peering at him with her left eye.

"We're doing the full five decades," Robyn hissed at him with a nod, then turned back to Sister Mary just as she started the prayer over.

"Hail Mary, full of grace," they said together.

With a sigh, Bert wandered off back up to the gaol entrance. Neither of the women stopped praying until he was gone and Robyn wasn't sure whether she should thank Sister Mary or the Virgin Mary.

"Good," Sister Mary said, although her voice was unsteady, "Now just use the other tool to throw the ball."

Robyn let out a deep breath and her hand was shaking as she slid the second L-shaped tool into the lock.

"Twist the other way," Sister Mary said, her voice was calm but her breathing was still uneven.

Robyn felt the resistance of the metal and, just as if she was turning a key, she twisted the tool around and the lock clicked.

They both froze for a moment. Staring at one another. Hesitantly, Sister Mary tried the bars with her elbow and the cell door opened. She laughed. "You did it!"

"I said it was simple," Robyn said with a shrug and a grin hidden by her stained rags. Relief washed over her making her giddy.

"Now what?"

Robyn's stomach twisted again. They didn't have much time, long enough for them to finish fifty Hail Mary's. She could cook a decent fish in half that time, so surely they had long enough. Surely? All they had to do was come up with a plan of action, sneak past the guards, then make a bid for freedom. Perhaps she should have said they were doing ten decades. Or a hundred.

She had to focus but her nerves seemed to prevent all rational thought.

Robyn knew she'd as good as put Sister Mary behind those bars herself. It was Robyn's fault she had suffered that hideous trial by ordeal. Robyn had thought it all no more than a game but now she saw how real it was. If Sister Mary was going to get out, there was only one thing they could do.

"You're going to walk out the front gate," she said firmly.

"What?" Sister Mary looked at her as if she had suggested they fly out, "you do know where we are, don't you? You do understand that they will kill me on sight?"

Robyn's stomach sank as she remembered Littlejohn's words of warning to her. But she shook her head. "They are not going to see you." She took off her tatty old cowl spilling some of the sheep wool onto the gaol floor and then hurriedly began peeling off the bandages. "They will only see Nora." She held up the filthy, stained rags, but the sister hesitated, seemingly unwilling to touch them even with her own bandaged hands. Robyn laughed. "It's not blood," she explained, "just rust stains."

"Oh," Sister Mary replied, "clever." She took the rags but still hesitated. "And what are you going to do?"

"Don't worry about me."

"Don't worry about you?" Sister Mary stared at her, mouth agape. "But what are you going to do?"

Robyn was surprised. She had expected the young thief to gratefully take her way out and run, never to be seen again. It reassured her to think that perhaps she had been right to stop and help this strange woman, perhaps there was goodness within her, at her core. "It's my fault," Robyn replied, firmly, "You are in here because of me, it's only right that I get you out."

"Are you sure about this?"

"Absolutely, I break out of this place all the time," she lied smoothly.

"And yet you've only just learned to pick a lock? Impressive." Sister Mary smiled.

"You need to get going," Robyn said, taking a deep breath and pushing away the emotions that were washing over her.

With her hands all but useless, Robyn had to help Sister Mary into the disguise. With the old, ragged robes on top of the nun's habit, she must have been weighed down and hot. Robyn hurriedly wound the bandages around her head and then placed the old cowl over the top, strategically pulling out some of the sheep's wool. She was almost indistinguishable from the old woman who had entered.

"This isn't going to work," Sister Mary said as Robyn handed her the basket.

"It is," she hooked the basket onto Sister Mary's arm but when it became clear that Sister Mary would not be able to hold, much less *use* the stick, she just threw that in the basket as well, "just wave as you leave" Robyn explained, "and if they speak to you just... just cough at them until they go away."

"Cough at them?"

"Would you interfere with a diseased old woman?"

"I see your point." The mound of stained rags nodded but held back a moment. "Right."

Robyn waved her off, they were running out of time. "It's all right, just go. Go!"

Sister Mary turned to leave then looked back. She seemed about to say something but was unable to speak.

Robyn smiled. "If you need a safe house, go to The Blue Boar Inn just beyond the northern gate."

Sister Mary nodded then moved off down the corridor.

"Don't walk!" Robyn hissed after her.

"Don't walk?"

"Shuffle," Robyn explained, "shuffle as if you are a hundred-and-eleven year's old."

"Right," Sister Mary said with a nod, but her voice betrayed her fear and as the old mound of rags turned, waving a gnarled, bandaged hand, Robyn's stomach swirled in apprehension.

"Good luck," Robyn whispered, knowing they would both need it now more than any time in their lives.

10

GAOL BREAK

The moment Sister Mary was gone from sight, Robyn felt as if she had been drenched by a bucket of ice water. *What now?*

Suddenly she heard a hacking cough in the corridor beyond the gaol and knew that Sister Mary must be getting interrogated by the young guard, Bert. She held her breath, her whole body froze waiting. The silence went on for too long.

What if it was all for nothing? What if Sister Mary hadn't been able to pull off the deceit? Had Robyn just condemned them both?

A shadow moved at the top of the stairs.

Someone was coming.

She still had Sister Mary's sword. She could take Bert by surprise. Knock him down before he raised the alarm.

Then what? How would she make it past the guard on the gate?

But it was too late, he was coming down the stairs, the light of his lantern glowing against the wall.

Robyn did the only thing she could think of; she hid.

Darting into the now empty cell, she eased the creaking cell door closed and hid in the corner holding her breath.

The cell would appear empty if he came too close. *Would he get too close?* She didn't know what he was looking for.

She clutched the handle of the sword. It wasn't her usual weapon. Her father had given her a few lessons on long summer evenings back when Loxley was a thriving manor, but she had always preferred her bow.

The leather soles of Bert's boots clapped against the flagstone as he drew closer. There was a hesitancy in his step. She could almost hear his nerves.

Briefly, a thought passed through her mind. Perhaps she could pretend to be Sister Mary. He might be convinced by her voice; she could remain hidden as if in shame and then when it came to the trial her hands would be healed as if by God. But she shut the thought down immediately. Even if she had taken the sister's habit, her face was known; she would be recognised. And the thought of spending three days pretending to be locked in an open cell while starving did not appeal to her.

She would wait until nightfall.

She could put the plan she'd intended for Sister Mary into practice.

Robyn heard a low muttering voice. She peered around the edge of the wall to look beyond into the corridor. Bert had paused to talk to another prisoner.

Perhaps that would be as far as he would go. Perhaps he wouldn't check on her. She could hide in peace until nightfall, and then slip out. Escape through a side door.

"Now, don't be thinking you'll be gettin' no more food," he admonished the poor, silent man before turning his attention back to Robyn's cell.

She darted back into her corner. Her back was to the wall, listening to him draw closer as she held her breath and clutched the sword. She could run the guard through and make a run for it.

But he was barely more than a boy, and she had been honest about his mother. *How could she ever face Martha at the Alms-house again after murdering the woman's son?*

"Where are you hiding?" Bert drew up to her cell, his fingers slid through the bars as he pressed his face up against it. If he pulled on the door it would open.

"No one should see me," Robyn stammered, hoping she'd mastered a rough approximation of Sister Mary's haughty voice.

"Ah now, don't say that," Bert replied, "you're a pretty thing, I know that much." He was pressing himself against the bars, pushing his hand through. "You was fortunate to get some food from old Nora, but don't you be thinking you'll be getting no more, or ale for that matter." He chuckled, darkly. "Although if you're willing to be nice to me, I might be able to fetch you a little something from the kitchens."

In an instant, her fear switched to anger. *How dare he? Had that been the fate awaiting Sister Mary? A new ordeal at the hands of this rugged, stupid boy?*

She clutched the sword tighter, stifling an urge to leap forward and plunge it into his gut. But as she did, an idea flashed into her mind and no sooner did it appear than she acted on it.

"Now, now, laddie," Robyn croaked, "I'll have to tell your ma that you made that kind of proposition, and to a woman of the cloth no less."

"N-Nora?" his voice was stained with a sudden terror, he pulled back from the bars, "I saw you leave!"

Robyn stepped out of the shadows and looked up at his confused face with a wide, satisfied grin. "Don't believe everything you see."

"W-witchcraft!" He didn't move, his mouth hung agape for seconds before he came to himself and rummaged for his sword. But Robyn was too quick for him. She grabbed hold of the door, using its sheer weight to batter into him as she opened her cell.

"Argh!" He cried out as the metal slammed into him. His hands went straight to his face and blood seeped through his fingers. "You've cracked me nose."

"Sorry, Bert."

He stared at her with resigned defeat as she raised Sister Mary's sword to his throat, circling him until his back was to the cell and hers was to freedom.

Blood trickled down his tunic as he muttered barely recognisable obscenities.

"Take off the armour."

He looked at her, his hands dropped to his side revealing a swelling crooked nose beneath. "God's arse!" he growled. He shook his head defiantly but Robyn gestured with the blade tip, nearing his neck.

He swore once again and then, like one of her tiny brothers, asked to give up his toys before bed, the young man threw down first his helmet, then the sword, bugle, and heavy bunch of keys, followed by his blood-splattered livery and mail. As he went to pull off his undershirt Robyn stopped him. The least she could do was leave him in his underwear and hose. The poor boy had suffered enough humiliation and she had little desire to see any more of him.

"Get in the cell."

He threw back his head and whined. "Oh but-"

"Think about it, Bert," she told him, matter-of-factly,

"they are going to want to know how the prisoner got away. Do you think they will believe you if you say she turned into an old woman and walked out in front of you? Or do you think it might be better if you tell them you were overwhelmed by Robyn Hood and his band of outlaws?"

He looked about to argue, but then the last of Bert's fight left him and he bowed his head and sighed. "Robyn Hood and his band of outlaws."

"Good lad." She stifled a laugh and wondered if the boy was even younger than the eighteen years he appeared. "Now, get in and we'll say you fought like a lion but were beaten back by numbers, alright?"

He nodded mutely as he entered the cell and she locked the metal door behind him with his own set of keys. He stood staring at her looking a little cold and sad with his bruised and bloody face.

"It might be better," she added thoughtfully, "if you slump on the floor as though you were knocked out."

"Yeah," he nodded and her stomach gave a jolt of guilt as she detected the faintest crack in his voice, "that's a good idea."

She watched him settle himself on the floor, trying a few times to get comfortable on the hard stone and she found herself unable to walk away. "I meant what I said, you know," she whispered as she picked up his scattered belongings.

"About Robyn Hood?"

"About your ma." He opened his eyes, staring up at her suddenly as if seeing her for the first time. "She's a good woman," Robyn continued, "I don't know where they'd be without her down at the Alms-house."

Bert offered a lopsided grin and nodded. "Thank you."

"No," she said with a gracious bow, indicating the gift of

his armour and sword, "Thank you, and remember, it was Robyn Hood and his rugged band of outlaws,"

"Aye," Bert said, lying back on the floor, and closing his eyes. "Robyn 'ood."

Robyn grinned, and hurriedly slid the heavy mail and livery over her own clothes and fastened the helmet and belt. She would sheathe one sword and carry the other, there was no harm in having two. It felt strange to be wearing the red with a green cross and crowns of Nottingham. From a distance, she might pass as one of the guards, but up close, anyone would recognise her face as a woman's; she was certain of it. *She would have to keep to the shadows and make sure she didn't run into anyone.*

She hesitated before she left and turned to the prone Bert one last time. "And another thing," she said, as he opened an eye to look up at her, "next time you have a woman in one of these cells, in fact, next time you have anyone in these cells, you might think about treating them the way you'd want your lovely ma to be treated, right?"

He pursed his lips together and nodded. All the man had gone out of him and it was just a child that Robyn left in that cage.

With a last check to make sure the tabard was sitting correctly and her new belt was tied properly, Robyn headed out of the gaol.

"Wait!" a voice called to her rough, and thirsty, "Wait! Let me out too, please!"

The unkempt man shuffled to the bars of his cell, reaching out for her. Robyn didn't know how long they kept prisoners in Nottingham gaol but it looked as though he could have been there for months. If not longer.

She hesitated; *she still had the keys. It wouldn't take a moment to unlock that cage, she could set him free. He would cause enough of a distraction for her to escape. But by the look of him, the distraction wouldn't be very long. They would run him down and run him through in moments. She would be free, but it would be at the cost of this man's life.*

She shook her head; it was a terrible idea.

"I beg of you." His voice was rough, dry and desperate. She couldn't tell how old he was beneath the beard and long hair but his eyes were bright and youthful.

Robyn knelt before him. "They will kill you, my friend."

"Then I shall die a free man today and not as a prisoner starving to death."

He was right. She was leaving him to die. Her hand grasped the keys. But surely there was hope. There was always hope. Littlejohn himself had been pardoned. Perhaps the same would happen to him, if she caused his death now, all hope would be lost. The memory of Theobald came back to her and she shook her head; the blood of one man on her hands was already too much.

"I'm sorry," she whispered and stood quickly, closing her eyes as he called after her. She knew his voice would haunt her.

Out in the castle grounds, a cold wind whipped up and reminded her that summer was over and winter would not long follow.

She scanned the grounds, the sounds of the new mysterious soldiers carried on the wind. There were so many, she couldn't outrun them all.

She could walk straight through the front gates but she wasn't certain she could pass unquestioned and her new disguise wouldn't stand close scrutiny.

Perhaps there was another way. She didn't know the castle well. Perhaps there was a postern door, a small side door just like the one she used to have back home at the manor of Loxley. Or perhaps she could sneak through the busy kitchens, they may be too troubled by work to pay much attention to her. She could make her way down to the castle quay... then what?

She would have to explore. She took a deep breath and checked her weapon. It was odd having a blade rather than a bow, but in a pinch, it might just save her life.

Skirting around the edge of the inner castle walls she kept an eye out for anything that could tell her where a postern door might be located.

Another guard was coming in the opposite direction. She glanced back. *Would it be too obvious to turn around and walk away? Should she just walk with purpose, and hope he paid no heed to her?*

Her face was bare; she couldn't hide it under her usual scarf but could she pass for a boy? Even if she did, would he still question who she was?

She passed a building and made a snap decision. Rather than face the guard, she slipped inside. As she sealed the door behind her, she breathed a sigh of relief and was greeted with the heavy stench of horse manure. She'd found the stables.

Good, she could linger a moment. Hidden.

She made a quick pass along the stalls, making sure there were no stable boys about. Then she stopped dead.

"Jasper?" She stared. Unsure for a moment. Then certain. It was him. His light chestnut hair, the small white diamond on his forehead, that familiar nickering. She walked over to him; it was her horse. The horse taken from Loxley manor by the sheriff's own bailiff. She should have known he would be here, but seeing him again, feeling the warmth of his hair beneath her hand; he was like something from another life. "It is you! How have you been, boy?" He nuzzled her hand. "Oh, if only you could talk, boy! You could tell me how to get out of here!" She laughed despite herself. "God's breath, look at us? I never thought I would see the day when we were both full-dressed in the livery of Nottingham!"

As soon as she said those words, an idea struck.

It was a mad idea.

It would put three lives at risk.

But there was the slimmest of chances that it might just work. She might save four lives today and not just one.

But if she was going to pull it off, it would have to be now, she couldn't risk Bert getting found before she was ready.

Like lighting, she grabbed hold of the saddle and tack, dressing Jasper hurriedly. None of the equipment was of the quality she would expect and she wasn't used to dressing her own horse. Her fingers fumbled in excitement and panic. But as soon as she was done, she edged him out of the stall and then stood back to admire him. Jasper whinnied in irritation.

"I know, I know," she whispered, "I'll be back don't worry," she held up her hand, telling her horse to stay put. Then she turned and hurried back out the way she had come.

"You are mad, Robyn," she whispered to herself as she half-walked-half-ran back into the very place she had escaped from minutes earlier.

Glancing behind as she slipped along the gaol corridor, she stopped at the cell and plunged the keys into the lock. The poor man grabbed her, renewed by the energy of freedom. He seemed to have regained the strength of a hundred men. He would need it.

"Thank you," he cried, shaking her, "Thank you!"

"Stop it," she said, throwing him off, "Stop it, listen to me, listen to me, what's your name?" she looked around, wary that any moment a guard could find them.

"Reynold, it's Reynold, but most call me Greenleaf."

"Right, Greenleaf, look at me, I need you to stay here-"

"No! Please I beg of you-"

"Listen!"

He stopped.

"Greenleaf, I need you to count to a hundred for me, can you do that?"

He looked at her wide-eyed, his mouth opened and closed for a moment, "A- a full one hundred...?"

"Hail Mary!"

"What?"

"Can you do ten Hail Marys?"

"Yes, yes of course but-"

"You are going to do ten Hail Marys, and then, and only then, you are going to run out of here, do you understand?"

He nodded, with wide, glinting eyes.

"You are going to run from here through the castle gates and all the way to... do you have anyone to go to?

"No, no... my father's dead."

"Then run to Sherwood. Hide in the forest. Do not look back for one moment. Do you understand?"

His jaw gritted, and he gave one sharp nod.

"Good. Now start, Hail Mary."

The young man started, and the moment he did, it was Robyn's countdown.

She bolted to the top of the gaol stairs, ran along the corridor and back out into the sunshine. She wondered if she should have said twenty; his life was now in her hands and relied on her ability to get her timing right.

She raced around the inner ballium, but she stumbled to

a halt as she noticed a group of guards in the strange gold and red colours she had seen in the woods. She couldn't afford to draw their eye, so despite the countdown, she walked, almost crying in desperation.

Finally, she slipped into the stable and breathed a sigh of relief that Jasper was still there, though he let out a sharp snort to let her know how little he liked the manner in which he was being treated.

Suddenly, there was a shout.

She had just run out of time.

Dammit, that man must have raced through those Hail Marys.

Robyn leapt onto Jasper and kicked him into a gallop.

They burst through the stable doors and she saw him, the rag-dressed young man darting like a jackrabbit for the gates, a man with a pike was in hot pursuit and another stood in his path.

But Robyn had Jasper.

Horse and rider darted after Greenleaf, and Robyn was thankful he was fast enough for her to feign a good chase.

"I'm on him!" she shouted to the pike-wielder, and the big-bellied man waved a grateful thanks to her as she passed. "Out of the way!" she cried, her hand waving furiously to the guard preventing the man's escape.

Obediently, the guard moved to let the prisoner through the gates quickly followed by the rider. *You had him, you fool!* she thought with a grin as she darted after the escaped prisoner, down the cobbled lane into the town of Nottingham and to freedom.

11

FREEDOM

After seeing Greenleaf safely off to the woods, Robyn sneaked through the back window of the bustling Blue Boar Inn. She was surprised to see the now-familiar costume of Nora seated at a small, round table in the corner. The Blue Boar's resident cat, Merry, sleek and black, was being paid far more attention than that useless mouser deserved and he leapt onto the table purring appreciatively as 'Old Nora' struggled to pet him with balled fists.

Robyn had been sure that Sister Mary would have run far, far away as fast as she could from all of Nottinghamshire. But she was also quite glad to see the intriguing thief again.

Robyn was still wearing her stolen guard's livery and although a guard in The Blue Boar was not an unusual sight, she decided to keep her visit brief. "I'm surprised you waited for me," Robyn whispered, slipping onto the stool opposite the sister.

"Dear lord!" Sister Mary said with a start, "I nearly leapt from my own flesh!" She shook her head but the bandages concealed her features and Robyn couldn't tell if she was pleased to see her or not. "I have nowhere else to go. Thanks to you, I'm wounded," she raised her bloodied and bound hands as if Robyn had somehow forgotten in the brief hour or so that had passed, "and penniless."

Robyn clenched her jaw. On the one hand, the woman was a thief who had attempted to steal everything she owned, and so any punishment she had received had been justice. But on the other hand, Robyn knew from bitter experience that there was little real justice in the law and her own foolery had been the real cause of the sister's wounds. Another outlaw might have left Sister Mary to fend for herself and given her a good clout for the trouble she caused, but Robyn was no ordinary outlaw.

"Can the Church offer you sanctuary?" Robyn asked hopefully.

"The Church?" Sister Mary scoffed, "It's the Church I am running from! Or did you not notice the fact that I am a nun?"

Now it was Robyn's turn to scoff. "A nun," she laughed.

Sister Mary looked at her, her one revealed eye was wide, and the attentive black cat now in the sister's lap seemed to turn his accusing eyes at Robyn in a mirror of the sister's. "Does that amuse you?"

"Well... I," Robyn's brow furrowed, and she shook her head incredulously, "But you're not a *real* nun."

"Am I not?"

"You're a scafflocke, a thief, you said so yourself."

Sister Mary shrugged. "It hardly matters, I can't go to the Church for clemency, and unless you can pay a doctor for both his herbs and his silence then I suppose we are both stuck here for the foreseeable future," Sister Mary attempted to stroke the cat with the back of her wounded hand, "no matter how appealing the company."

But Sister Mary's prophecy was immediately proven wrong the moment Merek entered the room and caught sight of Robyn.

"You again!" Merek wailed, "You hope to ruin an old man! See him hang from the gallows!" His hands opened in a desperate supplication to an absent god. "And what is this?" he asked, catching the cloth of her shoulder and roughly shaking the livery. "Please, Robyn, tell me you have joined the town guard for, if this is stolen-" he shook his head unable to contemplate the consequences, leaning upon a table and blessing himself dramatically.

"Apologies, old man," Robyn stammered as she stood. She was used to Merek's dramatics, but at that moment she felt responsible for the sister's safety and the feeling drained her humour. "I'm already leaving,"

"You were never here!"

"I was never here," Robyn added, with a slow nod and a sinking stomach. "Come on." Robyn added turning to Sister Mary.

"You're bringing guests now? Is this one an outlaw? Is she on the run? God preserve us." Merek turned his eyes to the ceiling and began furiously praying to the rafters.

"Where are we going?" Sister Mary hissed, "I thought this was your safe house?"

"I'll tell you on the way," she lied to the woman of the cloth and flashed her most reassuring smile, then turned back to Merek, "Any news on my bow?"

"Bow?" he cried, turning a weak shade of purple, "You leave it with me in the morning and expect news by noon? What Saint of Fletchers do you take me for? Out!" he shook a filthy rag as he bustled them toward the side door.

Robyn opened her mouth to ask if there was any food she could take with her, the hunger was starting to claw at her stomach, but as she did so Merek sent a second flurry of harassment and it was all she could do to leave the inn without being attacked with a broom.

As they stepped into the cool air Robyn could hear the church bells heartily peeling. It took her a few moments to realise that the sound was not the familiar chiming of noon; it was the hue and cry. The whole of Nottingham was being told there was an outlaw on the loose.

"So," Sister Mary said, desperately looking to Robyn, "What now?"

Robyn opened her mouth, thinking fast.

She still had Jasper. They could race into Sherwood and find Littlejohn then all hide in the woods until this blew over.

But what about Sister Mary's hands? If those blisters turned foul, she would get a fever and they had no way to help her in the depths of the woods. Even if she made it to one of the surrounding villages, the hue and cry would have reached them too and there would be no faces as friendly as Merek's or with more reason to take her in.

Every man, woman and child in the two counties would soon be on their tail.

Robyn shook her head. There was only one place she knew of where she could find aid *and* be safe.

But if she went there, she would be bringing the force of both the sheriff's law and canon law down on the head of the one person she loved more than anyone else in the world: Marian.

12

A NEW ORDER

"What time is it?" Even in his half-sleep, the sound of the bishop's rage could fill the room and rattle the window shutters.

"Two hours after noon, your grace," the velvet encased manservant bowed low, his tone was soft and his face impassive.

"And what work of the devil forces you to wake me at this ungodly hour?" He rolled onto his back still clutching the blankets tight around his shoulders.

"It is the young sister, sire, she-"

"She was dealt with yesterday." The bishop pulled the blankets up and went to roll back into a determined sleep.

"She has escaped."

"What!"

The young manservant took a well-practised step back as the blankets were thrown back and two legs wheeled around and landed on the floor.

"Damn my ankles," the bishop muttered, "where are my slippers, man?"

"Just here, sire," the young man kneeled and pushed the

slippers forward into the realms of the bishop's swollen feet. A hard and heavy hand pushed down on the young man's back as the bishop used his presence to lever himself off the bed.

"My surcoat!" he ordered.

The young man scrambled off the floor and hurried to fetch the rich, fur-lined garment, and held it up for the bishop to walk into.

"What time is it?" the bishop demanded.

"Two hours after noon," the manservant replied without a trace of irritation upon his lips.

The bishop nodded; a gentle snarl curled his upper lip. "Then Nottingham will be about." His voice had become a low growl and there was a crimson tinge to his cheeks. "Nottingham!" he cried, making for the door to his chamber. "NOTTINGHAM!" he shouted, getting louder as he drew closer to the source of his wrath.

The manservant dutifully followed, watching without comment or correction as the bishop blindly banged each door he came to with his round fist.

"Nottingham!" he cried, with each sharp round of banging before moving on from one door to the next.

The manservant wasn't certain if he did this in a genuine attempt to find the man, or if it was simply a way of letting the whole castle know of the bishop's anger.

In nothing but his shirt, surcoat and slippers, the bishop hurried out of the chamber block and marched into the yard. A cold October wind lifted his robes and the man stood blindly trying to pick out the right direction.

His manservant hurried to catch up with him. "This way, your grace."

"I've a good mind to hang that damned man from the town gallows," he grumbled as he marched after his servant, but the man knew better than to reply or, God forbid, offer his own opinion, "infernal incompetence, two escapes! Does the man keep a gaol or an inn?" he laughed at his joke, "did you hear that eh? Erm... man, young man? Did you hear? Does the man keep a gaol or an inn?" He laughed again.

The manservant stopped at the imposing door to the offices of the sheriff and turned to the bishop with a bow. "Very good, your grace. The offices of the High sheriff."

"What's that? Oh..." he appeared to remember the reason he had been so unceremoniously summoned from his slumber and the rage bubbled up within him once again causing his teeth to grind. "Nottingham," he growled.

The manservant heaved open the door as the bishop, in his raging tempest, marched through.

William sprang to his feet from the low, wooden chair in the corner as the bishop squinted around the room searching for moving figures.

"Nottingham!" The bishop bellowed at the desk, not realising it was Maud who stared up at him with a quill in her hand as she completed the final paperwork for the quarterly accounts.

"Good afternoon, your grace," William managed.

"Afternoon, Nottingham? Good afternoon? I retire for just a few hours of rest, and when I wake, I hear of nothing but your incompetence and you dare to say to me 'Good afternoon'?"

"Apologies, your grace," William stammered, "I see you have heard-"

"Heard? Of course, I've heard Nottingham. Did you

think I should sleep so soundly I would not hear of the escape of my prisoner?"

"Well, your grace, I... er..." William was utterly lost for words; he glanced at Maud but she knew better than to let her presence be known.

"What traitor let her go, Nottingham? Which of your men was in on it, or should I have them all strung from the castle walls?"

"None of them, sire," William said more firmly than he had expected of himself.

"None of them, Nottingham? None of them? Dare you tell me that she melted through the walls? Disappeared like a spirit?" Spittle was forming at the edge of his mouth as he rounded the table and drew close to William's shrinking frame. "That woman may be a demon but she is as solid as you or I and if you expect me to believe she escaped from here with no aid from anyone then I shall take it that you, yourself, were the one who set her free and I shall have you tried for her crimes in her stead."

"Robyn Hood," William stammered, "it was Robyn Hood."

"Robyn Hood?" The bishop asked, bemused.

"An outlaw, your grace, she- er - he..." William quickly corrected himself, "he has been plaguing these parts for weeks, sire, the people are terrified. He's a horse thief-"

"A horse thief?"

"Aye, your grace, and a highway robber,"

"Highway, eh?"

"Yes, your grace, he and his band have been growing in number, taking advantage of the king's absence. My own nephew was murdered in pursuit of the villain, my lord."

"Murdered? Indeed?" The bishop's milky eyes were wide in interest, although bereft of compassion.

"The rogue has been hiding in the woods, stealing chickens and harrying peasants throughout the shire." William was getting into his tale and there was no reason he couldn't pin every crime in the shire on one criminal, it would make solving the problem that much simpler. "But he has never dared take on the castle. But devils seek devils and no doubt outlawed men from far countries have joined his band after hearing his misdeeds."

The bishop blinked. For a moment it seemed he was so taken in with the notion that he had forgotten his original intentions. "Do you mean to tell me that a merry band of outlaws walked into this castle and took my prisoner, yet no one thought to stop him?"

"Robyn Hood stole a horse and armour. There was no reason to think he was anything other than a guard chasing down a prisoner."

"So, this Robyn Hood released the prisoners then left after them with a horse and livery stolen from your own stables, and your men did nothing but stand by and watch?"

William suppressed a smile as he replied. "As did your men, sire."

The bishop let out an exasperated burst of rage as his cheeks turned a dark crimson. "Scour the town," he shouted, "crawl through every inch! Find this man, use all your men and mine if you must, but bring me my prisoner! And bring me Robyn Hood." He turned to leave, no doubt expecting his orders to be followed to the letter.

"They have likely fled into the forest, your grace," William called after him.

"Then scour every inch of the forest," he cried, turning back and sending spittle halfway across the room, "Make them scour all day all night and then all day again tomorrow if they must!"

William paused for a moment, weighing up his options. In weeks he hadn't found that damned little weasel, but perhaps with access to the extra manpower, he might just be able to hunt that scoundrel down. He nodded firmly. "It will be done, your grace."

"And mark my words, Nottingham," the bishop added in a low growl, pointing firmly in his direction, "I shall have your position for this, if not your head." He turned and swooped out, slamming the door behind him.

Maud breathed out a long sigh. "I could have him killed, you know."

William burst out laughing.

"Do you think I jest?" she asked slowly, and although she was seated, she seemed to look down on him.

"No," he replied, wiping a tear as he shook off the laughter, "and I must have finally gone mad for I find that even more amusing."

Robyn and Sister Mary rode all through the afternoon and long into the evening. With two on the horse, the journey had taken far longer than expected and sticking to the forest tracks to avoid roads took longer still. A cold wind picked up. The sister's enthusiastic complaints simmered down to nothing and she held Robyn's waist just tight enough that Robyn was assured the young woman wasn't asleep.

The cold stars were scattered across a velvet blue sky, and Robyn wondered if she should risk setting up a camp for the night when she finally spotted the lanterns shining against the white walls of Leaford Manor high on the hill.

"There!" she cried and felt Sister Mary start behind her.

"Wha?" a sleepy voice replied.

"We're here," Robyn replied.

She was anxious. The Baron of Leaford was not necessarily an ally, no matter how long he had been friends with her father. It was only a few weeks ago that he had been one of the barons called to a jury that had condemned Robyn's mother for treason.

She knew she could be turned away if she met with him and decided it would be best not to risk a bold entrance. Instead, she would clamber inside in her usual way.

Robyn headed toward the west side of the manor. One of the towers had long fallen into disrepair and the exposed wattle gave her an easy route in. She had often snuck in late at night or early in the morning over the years. But for the last few weeks, she had been determined to avoid the place no matter how much it pained her.

As they drew closer, she realised that many of the white patches of old crumbling plaster had been repaired. Panic swelled in her stomach, and she held her breath, letting out a sharp sigh of relief as she saw her unconventional entrance was still there, albeit with much scaffolding and buckets of lime thereabouts. It wouldn't be around for much longer.

She halted Jasper and slid off her horse. "Wait here for me," she hissed at the sister.

"I'm not likely to wander off, am I?"

Robyn smiled at the reproach and shook her head, at least Sister Mary still had her sense of humour.

The old, unrepaired dawb filling between the wattle sticks crumbled as she began her ascent. The wall bowed slightly, wider at the bottom than at the top, giving Robyn a distinct advantage and she was able to scramble her way to the top with practised ease.

She landed on the wooden palisade silently and glanced

around. A few more lanterns burned here and there but she didn't need the lights to know where she was going. She could walk around Leaford Manor blindfolded.

She descended into the gardens and could hear the little bells of goats disturbed by her presence. She waited for the sound to pass and for the animals to settle once again before moving, silently as a shadow, toward the postern door.

The old, stiff lock long needed to be replaced, and she grunted as she fought with it. Finally, with a thud and the crack of metal against wood, she wiggled the rusty latch free and lifted the bar to open the door.

Sister Mary was there ready for her. "How is it that you can sneak so easily into this castle?"

"Oh, that's no trouble," replied Robyn with a grin, "the walls are crumbling and easy to climb, the baron has always been far too frugal to pay for repairs or nightwatchmen so-"

"Halt!" came a deep voice.

Robyn spun around and a lantern blinded her for just a moment.

She blinked but could make out a group of brutish, well-built men armed with pikes and dressed in the white livery with a red band of the baronage of Leaford.

They'd been caught.

"No nightwatchmen?" Sister Mary asked, in a sarcastic drawl.

"And what are we gonna do with you?" said a voice beyond the light, a voice she vaguely recognised but couldn't place.

"Oh," said Robyn raising her arms in submission, "I suppose I was wrong."

13

LADY OF LEAFORD

Robyn and Sister Mary were marched into the dark, long hall of Leaford Manor. There were no candles lit and the fire had long gone out. The only light came from the lanterns carried by the guards themselves.

Robyn wondered how to explain herself to Ranulf De Staynton, Baron of Leaford. His fort was brimming with men Robyn recognised from Nottingham castle, only now they wore the Leaford colours. She was a fool to come here. De Staynton had been one of the barons who'd proclaimed her mother guilty of treason. She should have known he would be in the sheriff's pocket.

"Fetch the mistress," a guard hissed to a startled servant girl who scurried away instantly.

Robyn's hopes soared. Rosamund De Staynton might yet be lenient upon her. The baroness was good friends with her mother, she may let them go and say nothing of the whole affair. Although Robyn would still be no better off; left out in the cold with a wounded friend and a party of guards on their tails.

A large, shaggy, grey-haired wolfhound ambled into the long hall.

"Alfred!"

At the sight of his old mistress, Alfred surged forward and was closely followed by a young woman in a long sleek gown. Her blonde hair was loose and wavy at her shoulders where she had clearly just taken out her plaits and her face was half lost in shadow.

"Marian!" Robyn went to leap forward but was hauled back by one of the guards.

"Hold it."

Marian stared at Robyn and slowly shook her head as if reprimanding a child caught with their hand in the honey pot. "You can let them go, Gil," she said with a lazy wave of her hand, "she is a friend."

"We found 'em sneakin' in the postern door, ma'am."

"Yes, well," Marian let out a long sigh and threw Robyn a disapproving glance, "she does that."

"All due respect, milady, but the baron told us-"

"The baron is not here, Gil, and whilst he is gone, I am your lord and master and I say you can let them go."

Robyn could feel the fist of the man twisting the cloth of her collar and not for the first time that evening, she wondered just how much danger she was in. "Yes, ma'am," the guard growled finally, before stepping back and lowering his weapon.

As Robyn felt released from his grip, she longed to run forward and take Marian into her arms, but Marian wasn't looking at her and she hesitated.

"You may take your men and go."

"But Milady-"

"Go!"

Robyn made no effort to suppress her grin as she glanced behind her and watched the surly men shuffle from the hall. The man, Gil, paused to give a broken-toothed snarl to Robyn. Now that she could see his face clearly, she remembered having several run-ins with that particular man in the summer. She nodded her farewell with pleasure.

As soon as he was gone, Robyn dashed forward. "Marian!" She lifted the slight young woman into an embrace but as Robyn went to place a gentle kiss upon her lips, Marian pulled away.

"Who is your friend, Robyn?" she asked pointedly, ignoring Robyn's quizzical look.

"Oh, this is just Sister Mary."

"Sister?" Marian couldn't hide her surprise, but she stepped forward and bravely held out a tentative hand to the bedraggled mound of rags that Sister Mary had become.

"This isn't my usual attire," Sister Mary said breezily as Marian's outstretched hand hung limply in the air between them.

"We need your help," Robyn said, carefully taking Marian's hand and lowering it as she added, "the sister is wounded."

"Yes, well..." Marian attempted a smile, "You obviously didn't come purely for the pleasure of my company."

A pang of guilt pierced Robyn's chest. She opened her mouth to launch into a thousand explanations but Marian had already turned to call out to the servant girl hidden in the dark corner. "Edyth, fetch some fresh linen and herbs if you would."

Once a fire had been lit in the brazier, and water brought out, the long hall of Leaford Manor started to feel much more like the home Robyn had always known it to be.

A bowl of hot water had been placed on the long hall feasting table, with balm, healing herbs and clean linen, then lady Marian set about unwrapping the wounded hands of Sister Mary. After much hissing, gasping, fussing and wincing, her blistered palms were soothed by the warm water and ready to be wrapped in the clean bandages.

"Where is your father?" Robyn asked, feeling a little surplus to requirements as she sat and watched Marian work.

"He went to London," Marian answered, without looking up, "he wanted to speak to the chancellor about your mother, but he was taken ill."

"Oh," Robyn stammered, unsure if she should ask more about the baron's intentions or his illness, "I'm sorry to hear that."

"It's quite alright," Marian said, finishing the bandaging and clearing up the old bandages, "he had a turn, but mother wrote to say he is back on the mend now."

"Thank you so much," Sister Mary's interruption prevented Robyn learning any more. She held her hands up looking at the fresh bandages in the light, Marian had done a far cleaner job of binding the wounds than whatever miscreant had attempted it before, and although Robyn opened her mouth to return to the subject of their parents, Marian had focused her full attention on Sister Mary.

"I can offer you some fresh clothes to get you out of those awful rags if you'd like?"

Sister Mary nodded enthusiastically. "Yes, anything."

"Wonderful," Marian smiled broadly, Robyn had missed that smile and seeing it again somehow made her ache and feel whole at the same time. "Come with me."

Marian headed off to the door without so much as a

backward glance and Sister Mary stood to follow, turning to Robyn. "Are you sure she's your friend?" she asked.

"Yes, of course," Robyn answered, startled that she would ask such a question.

"It's just that," Sister Mary shrugged, "she doesn't seem to like you very much."

14

A RECKONING

As Robyn went to follow the two women into the chamber block, Marian paused at the door. She glanced behind her into the gloom where Sister Mary had disappeared then finally looked up at Robyn. "Do you trust this woman?" Her voice was a low whisper, and Robyn had to lean forward to hear her words.

She nodded, then winced at her easy lie. "Well," she admitted, "she did steal from Littlejohn and me."

Marian raised her eyebrows and sighed; she opened her mouth to speak but merely shook her head.

"I do trust her though," Robyn added quickly, thinking of the young woman's vulnerability, how many times Robyn could easily have ended up in Nottingham gaol herself, and how it was Robyn's fault that the poor young nun had been captured by the sheriff's men and so badly wounded by a trial.

"Why, Robyn?" Robyn recognised that tone, it was the same tone that Marian had always used when Robyn had suggested they swim in a freezing cold lake, or travel to the next county on a whim, or ride their horses over ever-higher obstacles.

"I..." Robyn started to explain but her confidence and charm abandoned her. "I see something in her, something... like me."

"I see." Marian nodded, there was a bitterness to her smile that Robyn didn't recognise. "I had wondered why I hadn't seen you these last few weeks."

Robyn suddenly realised what the cause of her bitterness was and immediately tried to repair the damage. "No! It's nothing like that, I mean-I've only just met her...I - I haven't seen you because I didn't want to put you in danger. I'm still not clear of the sheriff's men, Marian, I couldn't risk leading them right to you."

"You risked it tonight."

"But...That's different; she needed help. I had nowhere else to go."

"And... I understand." Marian looked away and tried to shut the door but Robyn held it open.

"No, Marian, please, I wanted to protect you."

"I know." But she still wasn't looking at her and Robyn felt that with every word she said Marian was pulling even further away.

"I have been desperate to see you," Robyn whispered.

"Have you?"

She lowered her voice, all too aware of Sister Mary waiting for them in the room beyond. "I've thought about you every day we've been apart."

Marian sighed but she still didn't look up. "Have you?"

Robyn reached out to take her hand, *why was Marian slipping away from her? What could she do to bring her back?* "I've thought about our kiss."

Marian looked up then, and her eyes glistened. "Then

why-" she cut herself off as her voice cracked. "Then why have you not come to see me?"

Robyn opened her mouth but was unable to conjure a reply. She'd thought Marian would be delighted to see her again. Not driven to angry tears. "If I had put you in danger-"

"In danger?" Marian spat, "You think rescuing your mother from the clutches of the sheriff's men did not put me in danger?"

"Well, of course, but-"

"You think coming here tonight did not put me in danger?"

"B-but I-"

"So, you cannot put me in danger unless you need to put me in danger? You cannot risk coming here until you need to come here? You cannot risk doing anything until you need to do it?" Marian's cheeks were turning pink and her blue eyes seemed cold as stone. "What about what I need? All that time you say you have been thinking of me, but have you ever thought about what I need?"

"Well... I-"

"Have you ever thought I might be worried until I am sick with it? Thinking each day would be the day I would hear of your death? That every time I enter Nottingham it will be your body I see swinging from the gallows? Did you ever think of that?"

Slowly, Robyn shook her head, feeling the guilt writhe in her stomach. "I didn't."

"Did you ever think I might want to hear from you? I might want to know how you are? I might want to see you —" She choked on a sob, silencing her tirade and biting down as she looked away.

"I'm sorry," Robyn said, aghast and unable to think of anything else, "I had no idea."

"Of course you had no idea!" Marian hissed, "You never thought to ask!"

Robyn opened and closed her mouth several times. "I just wanted to keep you safe," she said, but her voice sounded weak.

But Marian shook her head. "It's not up to you to keep me safe. It's not up to you to decide when I should and shouldn't place myself in danger," Robyn opened her mouth to argue but Marian interjected before she could speak. "It's up to me." Marian stared at her and took both Robyn's hands in her own. "I thought I was your oldest, dearest and closest friend-"

"You are!"

"But you trust strangers more than you trust me. This Sister Mary of yours and that giant Reynold Littlejohn-"

"Littlejohn is a good man."

"I'm sure he is Robyn, but it still hurts that you trust him more than you trust me."

"But Marian I...."

"What?"

"I couldn't bear it if anything ever happened to you because of me."

Marian shook her head and looked up at her. "And I can't bear being cut out of your life like this."

"I love you, Marian."

Marian took a deep breath and nodded. "I know," she whispered, "But... what does that mean to you?" Marian waited a moment for Robyn's reply and when it didn't come, she shook her head, and stepped back, shutting the door in Robyn's path.

Robyn lay her hand and then her head on the wood as

she heard the bolts close. "It means everything," she whispered.

Candles flickered as the wind howled around the stone corridors of Nottingham Castle.

A half-sleeping guard started with fright at a sudden heavy knock on the small wooden door. He hesitated, but the knock came again. Glancing around in vain for another guard on duty, the young man stepped forward tentatively.

"Who goes there?" he called, clutching his pikestaff nervously. His question was answered with a further hard bang and this time it didn't let up. The young man hopped from one foot to the other, then relented and loosed the beam, opening the door slowly and looking out into the gloom beyond. "Oh, it's you!"

The young guard pulled back the door, letting in an older man who growled in thanks and shook out his cloak revealing the white livery with a red band of Leaford.

"Come back for your old job, Gil?" Bert asked with a grin.

Gil laughed. "If they doubled the wages and cut the hours it still wouldn't match it, no," he shook his head and glanced around conspiratorially, "I've come with news..."

"News?"

"News that the sheriff might want whispered in his own ear, Bert lad."

But the young man shook his head, wincing slightly as he did. "The sheriff's mighty pissed at you lot, all leaving as you did."

"The sheriff will want to hear this," Gil insisted.

"I dunno," the boy breathed heavily and looked around

desperately for another guard to come and relieve the burden of his decision.

"I know where she's hidin', Bert."

The younger man's head snapped back. "Who?"

"Robyn Hood."

15

THE HUNT

Robyn was slumped in the baron's chair. She had spent an awkward night on the hard ground by the cooling brazier tossing and turning as she thought over her conversation with Marian.

Her argument with Marian, she corrected herself.

They had argued. They had never argued before; they had bickered, teased one another, fought playfully over games... but argued? Really argued? Never.

It hurt.

The pain gnawed at her stomach, and her jaw clenched as a headache worked its way up her shoulders and neck to her temples.

During the rest of the long night alone, Robyn had grown tired of the clay beaten ground and pulled herself to sit in the high-backed baron's chair. If the lord of the manor wasn't here and no one else was in the hall, what did it matter if she defied convention and sat in the chair?

Robyn was finding that the more days she spent away from society, the less time she had for its conventions.

She had leaned forward over the brazier, occasionally

poking the fire with the tip of the sword stolen from Bert, the hapless Nottingham guard. But all she had managed to do was break up the burning logs sending white ash over the bare clay of the floor and causing the fire to cool far sooner than it would have.

Eventually, she sat back, pulled a cloak that she found tossed over the back of the chair around herself, then twisted into an awkward slumber, unsure if the distant noises and rushing figures before her were real or visions of sleep.

A sudden bark startled her awake. Alfred, her father's wolfhound, sat at her feet. They stared at one another for a moment before a heavy leather pack was tossed into her lap.

It winded her and she grunted in surprise.

Marian rushed past freshly dressed in a light green gown, with long plaits down to her waist as if her hair had grown a yard in the night. "I said, they're coming, Robyn!"

"What?" she asked, struggling to find her voice. "Who?"

"The sheriff's men, and the bishop's men along with them." Marian dashed past her again, this time in the opposite direction and followed by a pretty young woman with raven black hair, in a scarlet gown. It took Robyn a moment to realise it was Sister Mary. She assumed that Sister Mary had got dressed before anyone knew there were guards on the way as red was not the best colour to wear during an escape.

"Right," Robyn said, standing, "Right," she repeated, having no idea what to do. Then the panic filled her; the sheriff's men were coming. Along with the bishop's.

Which bishop? She had no idea, but if the men were seeking an outlaw, they would find two when they arrived. "We have to go!"

"That's what I've been saying," Marian snapped. "Come along, the horses are waiting."

She followed Marian out into the yard, slinging the pack over her shoulder and looking around to get her bearings in the bright sun. A boy stood patiently with Robyn's horse, Jasper, and Marian's black and white mare, Isolde.

"We won't need two," Robyn said, "Sister Mary cannot ride with her hands as they are, she can ride with me."

"My hands are far better than they were." The sister no longer looked anything like a bandaged beggar or a bitter nun. She had washed and her soft black hair was combed and loose to her shoulders, her green eyes sparkled and the gown Marian had given her, a touch too small, clung to her figure.

"Sister Mary *is* riding with you," Marian replied, hopping easily onto her own mount. "And I shall follow on Isolde."

Robyn stared. "No." She shook her head vehemently, but Marian shrugged.

"This is not your choice, Robyn."

A bugle sounded in the distance. The guards were drawing closer.

"You two can argue all you wish," Sister Mary said, hauling herself awkwardly onto Jasper.

But Robyn wasn't listening, she was looking up at Marian, a hand tentatively on the young woman's knee, pleading with her. "It isn't safe, they could hurt you, kill you, take you prisoner..."

"Please Robyn," Marian looked down at her, with both an equal measure of rage and sorrow in those blue eyes, "either you keep me in your life, or you let me go... completely."

Robyn shook her head; she couldn't believe she was

hearing Marian utter these words. "You are asking to become an outlaw Marian."

"I'm asking to be a part of your life."

Robyn almost gave in, at the piercing blue eyes that she loved with every part of her being, pleading with her, she almost gave in. But the danger was too real, Sister Mary's wounds were testament to what they would do if they even suspected Marian, and the gallows were testament to what they would do if they were certain. "No, absolutely not." The thought of seeing Marian hanged, or even injured… Robyn couldn't bear it.

Marian leaned down; she rested her hand upon Robyn's. "It hurts too much not to be with you," she whispered, "not knowing when or if ever I will see you again. I can't," she shook her head, "I refuse to go on like that."

"You'll see me, I'll make more time for you, I promise-"

Another bugle blared in the distance and that was too much for Sister Mary. "Damn you both," she called out, before riding through gates of Leaford Manor.

Robyn backed away from Marian, intending to take off after the sister on foot.

"If you walk away now, Robyn," Marian called after her, "if you leave me now, then don't you come back." Marian's voice was firm, but there was a tremble to the hand that held the reins of her horse, and her eyes glistened. "Don't you ever come back."

Robyn stared. Marian didn't mean it. She couldn't mean it. The third call of a bugle reminded her how close the men were. She wavered between capture and escape.

It was foolish to take Marian with her. It was foolish to put the woman she loved in danger. It was foolish to endanger herself further by adding Marian to her group. It was foolish. Too foolish to risk.

"Then what are we waiting for?" Robyn said, finally able to tear her eyes away from Marian, "let's go, let's go."

Robyn swung on to the back of the horse, and Marian tore off though the gates following the scarlet figure of Sister Mary upon Jasper.

16

SHERWOOD

Marian's horse was slow from carrying two people. Sister Mary tore ahead, she was barely a patch of red in the distance as the men drew closer.

"The sister!" Marian cried, "we shall never keep up!"

"Let her go," Robyn replied, thinking how much trouble she had brought upon the poor woman's head, and sympathetic with her reasons for heading off, "she owes us nothing."

But Robyn was looking behind.

Four men had broken away from the group storming the castle. And they were closing in.

One was drawing even further ahead of the others; he must have spotted them first and now he was closing the gap so quickly that Robyn could pick out the white star on his gold and red quartered tabard. She recognised these soldiers. "We have bigger problems," she replied.

Marian pushed the horse to go faster. Sister Mary was far ahead, darting into the forest already her scarlet gown disappearing into the thickness of the wood. If they could only get to the safety of the vast forest, they would soon lose their enemies, but not if they were too hot on their heels. With two riders on her back, Marian's poor Isolde just wouldn't make it.

"I'm weighing you down," Robyn said, casting her eyes desperately from their destination to their enemy in hot pursuit.

"We'll make it," Marian called back, more confident than their situation deserved, "together," she added firmly as if she knew exactly what desperate thoughts that were running through Robyn's frantic mind.

But it was no good. If either of them were to get away they needed to lose a rider and Robyn had an idea of just how to do it.

"Slow down," Robyn called.

Marian glanced back, her deep blue eyes wide in alarm. "Don't you dare," she hissed.

"Save the horse," Robyn replied, her voice steady despite her nerves, "you must," she added her voice above a whisper close to Marian's ear.

Whether through Marian's compliance or her horse's exhaustion, their pace was slowing, and the first man was catching up fast. They were all just a few yards from the tree line and closing in, the other men with less agile mounts were not far behind and Robyn knew that Marian's life and freedom depended on what she was about to do.

Suddenly the man was upon them. For what seemed like minutes they rode side by side. Marian glanced sideways and Robyn heard her sharp intake of breath as the man reached out to grab the reins from her hands. They fought for a moment each pulling and causing their horses to slow. It was now or never.

"Don't look back," Robyn hissed, then she jumped.

Grabbing the man's shoulders, Robyn landed squarely

behind him on the horse's rump. Instantly, he relinquished the reins and his thick leather gauntlets groped blindly behind his head for Robyn.

With one hand she grabbed his gold and red tabard to hold herself steady, with her other she tore the helmet from his head and swung it back around to collide with his bare face. With a yelp of shock, he grabbed at the helmet and she let him take it, then a swift heave to his back was enough to unbalance him from his mount.

He tumbled away and the horse reared, it was only luck that Robyn caught the reins as they swung wildly. She slipped into the saddle and without daring to look behind her at the cursing soldier she dashed after Marian into the trees.

Robyn noticed the swell of relief in Marian's eyes as she glanced behind and saw it was Robyn in pursuit. But her relief was swallowed by a grim frown and Robyn knew that despite entering the forest they hadn't shaken their tail.

"Where to?" Marian asked, quickly turning her eyes back to the path ahead as Robyn drew up alongside.

"Follow me." Robyn darted ahead, she knew these forest paths and if they could just shake their pursuers then they could reach her camp and hide for a while.

Robyn glanced back. But Marian's horse was falling further behind her and a guard was drawing ever closer. With a flick of her hand, Marian urged Robyn onward, but Robyn couldn't leave. She halted.

The man, with only his knees to hold him in the saddle, reached out grabbing Marian's reins with one hand and drawing his poniard with the other.

Robyn gasped as her stomach twisted in shock. But before she could swoop in to save her, Marian had yanked his sword arm, hard, then quickly punched it back. Hitting the man in the face with his own pommel. With no hand on his own reins, he flailed then fell.

Now with two horses, Marian dashed past Robyn. "Come on!" she admonished.

There were two more riders in pursuit and although the women could hear the horses and caught the occasional flash of red and gold through the trees, they couldn't seem to shake them.

"Woah!" Marian halted and Robyn caught up with her at the edge of a surging river.

"My God," Robyn said, staring at what had been barely more than a babbling brook two days before, "all that rain!"

"What do we do?"

Robyn glanced desperately up and down the bank trying to think where the best place might be to ford.

"There they are!"

The shout from behind forced them into action and, with no more than a panicked glance between them, they agreed on a plan and dashed into the ice-cold swell, leaving the freshly stolen horse alone on the bank.

Boots, then thighs, saddles and waists went under. Robyn gritted her teeth as the cold burned and her new horse protested.

A strange plop next to her startled her for a moment and she realised it was a bolt from a crossbow barely missing her. She glanced at Marian, unwilling to panic her. They were just feet from the far edge. As their horses clambered out of the muddy bank on the far side the young women were relieved to see the men behind them hesitate.

One she recognised, a man with a young face but a white beard, he gave them one last look and turned, galloping off. But Robyn's relief was quickly quashed when the other man entered the water, his gaze steady and unnerving.

"Come on," Robyn said, cold and tired of the chase, "we can deal with one more." She turned, pushing her horse into a canter, unwilling to punish the beast further and as Marian rode alongside her, Robyn hissed out her instructions. "Let him come between us."

She drew away and Marian seemed to understand, widening their gap as the last horseman closed in. Choosing Marian to pursue, he was quick to catch up with her, but she was ready. And it was his reins that were grabbed.

Suddenly Robyn was on his right side. They squeezed the guard's horse between their own preventing him drawing his weapon but Marian could draw hers. With a swift flick of her wrist, her sword was cutting at his taut reins but he grabbed at it. They flailed together fighting for the precious weapon for only a second before he wrenched it from her hand.

In a panic Robyn lashed out, swinging her fist and colliding hard with his nose. His head snapped back and he cried out. The blood was instant.

"Sorry!" Robyn stammered at the sight of his wound. He stared at her wide-eyed before she remembered herself and struck again. Marian, with a firmer grip on the horse's reins, pulled the beast away, while Robyn reached out grabbing a fistful of his red and gold tabard, pulling the man toward her as his mount departed. He flailed out to grab her, and she let him go expecting him to tumble to the ground. But his foot was caught in the stirrup.

He cried out as he was dragged helplessly along the forest floor, his stolen sword lost as he tumbled and rolled. Her sword out in a flash, Robyn reached out to cut his binding. A hand on her own reins and an eye on the forest path, she swung once too wide. He cried out as his body was driven roughshod over brambles and branches. She reached out again, the tip of her blade perilously close to the horse's flank, then snap. She was through the strap and the man was released.

They surged on with the freshly stolen beast, and Robyn was relieved to glance back and see the man alive and writhing on the ground; she couldn't bear another man's death on her conscience.

Her camp was not more than a half-mile further along the river and, free from pursuit, the two riders and three horses made the journey in minutes. Robyn dismounted as she headed toward the clump of trees and shrubbery that, at a casual glance, appeared impenetrable.

"Robyn!" Marian called suddenly, "Look out!"

But Robyn didn't have a chance to 'look out' as the whole weight of Marian dived upon her, knocking her heavily to the ground just at the sound of a heavy thud in a nearby trunk. The two women stared at one another for the briefest moment; their bodies pressed heavily against each other and their breathing upon one another's lips.

Marian was up in an instant, her hand went to her scabbard, but her sword was gone. Robyn dashed to her feet, pulling her own sword and searching the forest for their enemy. The white bearded rider, the man they thought had abandoned the chase at the river, was grinning as he reset his bolt. She rushed him, desperate not to let him load the deadly weapon. His horse reared and she fell back but Marian was ready to take up the fight. Armed with only an unsuitable branch she thwacked him once, then again and again. The man grabbed at the foliage, fresh leaves rained down from their battle before he let out a wild cry of humiliated fury and dismounted. He grabbed the branch, tearing it from Marian's grasp and tossing it aside in disgust. Defenceless, she backed away but the defiance didn't drop from her lips.

"Leave her be!" Robyn shouted, back on her feet, her weapon drawn and the blade tip pointed at him.

He turned, slowly, as if he knew she wouldn't run him through. He seemed taller now that they both stood rather than rode and there was a snarl of frustration on his lips as he drew his own sword.

"You're not makin' this easy," his voice was a low growl.

"Well, that would be no fun," Robyn replied, there was no gaiety to her tone and it took all her strength to ensure there was no fear in her voice either. Though she quaked in her boots and prayed to all the saints and the Mother Mary herself that Littlejohn would appear at any moment to save the day.

The man took a step forward. Instinctively, Robyn took a step back to match and she was certain that she saw a smirk curl at the side of his lip.

He took another step. She held her ground, though she had to fight every flighty instinct to do so.

Suddenly he jerked forward and with a gasp, she stumbled back a few steps, nearly losing her balance as he let out a roar of laughter.

She snapped. His laughter ignited a rage and suddenly she was upon him, a first strike, a second, a third, he was on the back foot, parrying her frantic attack. His merriment switched to surprise and then as soon again to determination as the strength and skill of a trained soldier outmanoeuvred the eager novice.

Thwack.

A fresh branch collided with his head, this time a stronger, thicker branch and the clang of wood against the metal of his helmet startled even Robyn. The man let out a yell of frustration as he grabbed the branch from Marian, but she held fast. He pulled, then suddenly pushed it just as hard and she fell back. He only just managed to parry the strike that Robyn levelled at him but he was done with the fight and with one flick of his wrist Robyn's sword had left her hand and he was bearing down upon her with not a shadow of mercy in his eyes.

As he raised his blade to strike, Robyn could only raise an arm in defence, but she was saved by the clang of another sword intercepting his.

She looked around in relief for Littlejohn, better late than never. But her mouth hung open as she saw it was Sister Mary, not Littlejohn who was expertly taking on the guard.

Armed with two swords, her own and Robyn's, Sister Mary parried every strike and quickly outmanoeuvred him. The poor man could parry one sword, but against the whirlwind of two expertly wielded blades, he was helpless. He fell back a step, then another, and then suddenly his own sword was flung from his hand.

Robyn rolled out of the way as the blade came flying in her direction, landing tip first in the ground.

She drew it and stood just in time to watch Sister Mary, her blades like scissors to his neck. There was a moment when Robyn was sure she would strike, then she pulled back, and tossed a weapon to Marian, while still holding her own sword to his throat.

"Do you wish to die today, friend?" she asked, although it didn't sound like she was giving him the option.

"They'll have you all hanged for this!" he snarled.

Robyn couldn't tell if the pleading in his voice was for their sakes or his own.

"They'll hang you first." Sister Mary hissed her words, and there was a level of enmity in her tone that unsettled Robyn. "For your failure."

"But don't worry!" Robyn stepped between them, forcing a grin and a jovial tone. "We'll say nothing if you won't." She turned his sword in her hand and offered him the hilt.

He held her gaze for a long, silent moment in which Robyn held her breath as tightly as she held her smile. Then he took the proffered handle and turned to storm away to his horse. He clambered the mount, seemed about to say a parting word, but instead steadied his horse and galloped away.

Robyn almost collapsed with the relief of it before she turned to the outraged faces of her companions.

"How could you return his sword?" Marian demanded, "He could have killed us all!"

She shook her head, suddenly exhausted. "He was still outnumbered and if we'd kept it, he would have had to explain the loss."

Marian let out an exasperated sigh. "I still think it was foolish."

"What else could we have done? We couldn't kill him."

"I could."

Robyn and Marian both turned to stare at the dark-haired woman in the scarlet gown who had saved them by wielding two swords better with wounded hands than either of them could wield one.

"Exactly what kind of a nun are you?" Marian demanded.

Sister Mary sheathed her sword and cradled her freshly bleeding hands. "One that's on your side."

17

REWARD

The camp had been raided.

The lean-tos had been torn to pieces, the sturdy wooden branches snapped and the furs and hides sliced to ribbons. Their ale had been poured out, and the clay bottles smashed, the food was gone, and the wooden chests shattered. A rank smell of burning fur lingered in the air where a torch had been thrown into the wreckage and still smouldered despite the damp morning mist.

Robyn looked around the desolation of her little home and her stomach seemed to fall to her feet. "Littlejohn," she whispered.

She rushed forward and began tearing through the wreckage desperately searching for something she hoped she wouldn't find.

"He's long gone," the dry voice of Sister Mary announced as she wandered around the camp, kicking bits of broken wood.

"They've taken him!" Robyn cried; her voice strained by panic.

"He may yet have evaded them," Marian said, taking Robyn's hands in her own.

Robyn nodded. *He was a strong man, capable. He would have been careful. He would have got away. He must have got away.*

"Well, wherever he's gone, he's got our money." Sister Mary emerged from the bushes and threw a broken lock down at Robyn's knees. It was the lock from her own chest. The chest that Sister Mary herself had picked. And the chest that contained her stolen silver as well as the fortune in gold the nun had been carrying with her.

Robyn stared at it mutely, unable to begin to comprehend the loss.

"Where would he have gone?" Marian asked, trying to shake Robyn back into the present.

"I... erm..." Robyn couldn't think, her mind was clouded; *if the guards had the money, they must have Littlejohn, he'd be taken to the castle gaol. Or worse, he may have been taken into the deep dungeons in the bowels of the castle. Could she make two rescues in one week? They surely would be ready for her this time.*

"The Blue Boar," Sister Mary announced, "That is your safe house, is it not?"

Robyn nodded. *Would Littlejohn have gone there?* "Yes," she said firmly. If he was alive, that's where he would have run to. She tried not to dwell too long on the 'if'.

"Right," Marian said, standing, "then that is where we must go. Where is this Blue Boar of yours? A village? A forest turnpike?"

Sister Mary looked at Robyn with an arched eyebrow and a rueful smile. "Oh, it is in a very safe place, isn't it, Robyn?"

"Nottingham? We're going back into Nottingham?"

"It is the last place they'll look, Marian."

"And a guard's tavern, at that, Robyn! You are mad, quite mad." Marian shook her head, "surely it is safer for us all to stay hidden in the forest?"

The three of them trotted along quite slowly, half-listening for pursuers, and keeping to the maze of well-worn paths that crisscrossed throughout the forest. Since the recent rain made it impossible to avoid leaving tracks then they had to leave tracks where they could not be picked out from the dozens of others.

"These woods are crawling with those men," Robyn said, looking around and half expecting their pursuers to come upon them, "they will never expect us to go back into Nottingham. And we have to find Littlejohn."

"And my money," added Sister Mary.

It was a long morning ride. They kept a steady pace so as not to tire their horses, but they daren't stop for a rest. At a distance, they would appear as two young women in the company of a rather lithe and scruffy guard of Nottingham town, and those who hadn't seen them already would know no different unless they came too close.

But the morning was fresh, bright and cool. The sun was bright through the trees and although they had no food or drink to sustain them through the morning, it was a pleasant journey and Robyn could almost forget she was an outlaw on the run and not just a baron's daughter out for a morning ride with friends.

At the sight of the white walls of Nottingham town, the

twist of nerves in her gut reminded her all too quickly of the danger. The three of them left the main road and headed down an ambling track away from the main gates and toward the higgledy-piggledy streets of the outer town.

"He's here!" Robyn said, trying not to let out a cry of joy and relief as she surged forward. In the backyard of The Blue Boar were the familiar dour features of Sister Mary's reluctant grey donkey, alongside Merek's friendly little brown mule. "Where's your new master?" Robyn asked, stroking the soft hair on the donkey's muzzle once she had led her own stolen mount toward the water trough.

"Will they be alright here?"

The backyard of The Blue Boar Inn was hidden by the encircling buildings, only their friends would be out here. However, it was smaller than the stables at the front and five beasts were a bit of a squeeze. "Safe enough for now."

Careful of guards on patrol, Robyn led them to the side door, she wasn't sure either Marian or Sister Mary would appreciate her usual entrance of the back window.

As Sister Mary entered, Marian called Robyn back quickly. "What is it?"

Marian was standing in front of the large notice board, filled with missives for those who could read and pictures for those who could not. "Look."

Marian pointed to the top row of images. Wanted posters with woodcut images and a figure for the reward. One of them was a dark-eyed, sharp-featured man whose cruel, twisted mouth frightened her even on parchment.

"Guy of Gisbourne," Robyn read, "I wouldn't like to meet him on a dark night. Or a bright afternoon for that matter."

"No, this one," Marian pointed to the top left corner, but Robyn was distracted by one just above her. A hooded figure, with a scarf and cruel eyes, 'Robin Hoode' was written above her own twisted image and she reached up to pull down the poster. "I'm only worth fifty silver," she shook her head, "I've spent more than that on a summer gown."

"That's the price for your corpse, Robyn, be careful about wishing the reward were higher."

"You two!" Merek hissed at them sticking his plump reddened face out of the side-door, "Why are you just standing there? Do you wish the world to see you? Do you want to bring the town guard down on my head?" He hurried them inside as he continued to reprimand them, "Here we were, fretting for your lives and you stand there like pigeons waiting to be plucked! My heart!" He added, clutching his chest and dabbing his brow with a cloth, "It cannot take it, it cannot take it I tell you!"

"It's good to see you too, Merek."

"And another young lady," he bowed and greeted Marian in between bouts of reprimanding Robyn, "how many young ladies are you going to bring to me? All these young ladies! You will be the death of me, you will all be the death of me."

Robyn tried to conceal her grin as they were shuffled into the dark and empty tavern. Lunchtime was long passed and it was not yet late enough for supper or revelling. Only a few figures hung low over tankards, but there was one figure in particular, she was looking for. "Is he here?"

"Oh yes," Merek replied, his voice low and dark, "and he will eat me out of business, that man. He eats when he frets and he has been fretting since dawn."

Merek led them up some creaking stairs to his own rooms above the tavern. "Any word on my bow?" Robyn asked.

"Always the bow, the bow, do you want miracles?"

"No, just my bow."

Light from the downstairs lanterns shone through the cracks, and the lantern Merek held burned bright, but it was barely enough to light the room and it took Robyn a moment to see the giant of a man, tankard in hand, who stood at their entrance.

"Littlejohn!"

"Ah, Rabbit! All safe and sound then?"

"Who are all these men, Merek? Have you finally brought a horde of assassins to do away with me? Can't even be bothered to do that yourself?" A grey and tired voice croaked from the corner and a pile of shadows shuffled and sat up in the dark.

"Mama?" Merek hurried over and lit a rushlight. "I thought you were sleeping?" He spoke as if to a child as he arranged the blankets back around the woman.

"How can I sleep with the king's army marching through my rooms?"

"'Tis the Lady Robyn, Mother-"

"Lady Robyn? What Lady Robyn? Robert is a man's name!" She sounded horrified at the prospect, and Robyn stepped forward and curtseyed, treating the old Innkeep with the same respect she would any dowager duchess.

"I was named for my father," she explained, "Robert Fitzwarren, Baron of Loxley. He left for the crusades not long since."

Merek's mother looked her up and down with a grim and piercing countenance. "Well," she said with a nod of her head, "That's a very ugly gown."

Robyn glanced down at the Nottingham heraldry of her stolen livery, it was muddy and torn in places. "Yes," she nodded, "it is."

The old woman pulled the blankets tighter around her

neck and seemed placated for the moment. Merek nodded to Robyn and with a last dazzling smile, Robyn turned away and went back to Littlejohn, slapping him on the shoulder as hard as she could manage. "So, how did you escape, old man?"

"I'll have less of the 'old man' thank you," he said gruffly, but his warm smile told her he was just as reassured to see her as she was to see him. "Them clumsy soldiers disturbed me in the night and I made off with a whiskers breadth to spare, but I had no chance to check on...the chest." He added the last bit quietly.

"Smashed," Robyn replied, remembering the worst news she had to break.

"And the contents taken," Sister Mary added.

"But thank God you made it away with your life, Reynold, that at least is something to be thankful for." But Marian's words did little to soften the blow. He sat back heavily in a chair.

"All gone..." he shook his head sadly.

"So, they got what they wanted," Merek said, joining them at the table. "No doubt they'll be gone now."

"Is that what they wanted?" Robyn asked, "I never knew what they were after. Unless they are all here for you?" Robyn looked to Sister Mary who didn't return her chuckle.

"So many men in the woods, scouring," Littlejohn shook his head, a low mood had descended upon him that Robyn didn't care for. "I've known naught like it since I were a boy."

"King Stephen's time," Merek added somberly and the two elders exchanged a glance that carried a cold dread twisting Robyn's stomach.

"But why here, why now? What do they want?" she asked.

Suddenly Marian threw a parchment poster down onto

the table, the word murderer was written above the name 'Wilfreda Gamwell' and the woman underneath had an arched eyebrow and a smirk as if she were an evil twin of Sister Mary.

Marian looked at Robyn pointedly. "They want her."

18

WILFREDA GAMWELL

Everyone turned to look at her. This young woman Robyn had known as the haughty Sister Mary, now stood before her, revealed as the liar, thief and murderess Wilfreda Gamwell.

"Is this true?" Robyn asked, knowing full well that it was, but wanting to hear Wilfreda's explanation. Or her denial.

"It would explain all the new soldiers hereabouts." Littlejohn had moved to stand behind Robyn's shoulder but she didn't turn to look at him. She didn't look at anyone else, she kept her eyes firmly fixed on the sharp, green eyes of the raven-haired Wilfreda, waiting for her to answer.

Wilfreda looked away, let out a long sigh, and then sat at the table. She didn't appear defeated or caught in a trap. If Robyn had to put a word to it, she would say that Wilfreda simply looked 'resigned'.

"Will you hear me out?" she asked, looking back up at Robyn as if she knew instinctively that Robyn was the only one whose permission mattered.

"Of course," Robyn replied, glancing briefly at Merek who let out a pained sigh.

"Then I shall tell you my tale, and..." she opened and closed her hands as if stretching out the still tender wounds, then shrugged, "if you are still set against me, so be it."

Robyn looked around the barely lit room. The eyes of her friends were wide and wary. She knew they would hear out the young woman. But there was no way of knowing how any of them would feel once her story had been heard. Her eyes settled on Marian; her face was half in shadow but Robyn caught a mild nod. Despite Marian's suspicions, she was ready to hear the young woman's story.

"Go on," Robyn said.

"My parents died when I was young," she said the words flatly and with little emotion, "I don't say this to gain sympathy it is simply the way it was, and I was far too young to remember either of them anyway." She shook her head and breathed deeply and Robyn couldn't help but feel that there was a torrent of emotion that she was forcing herself to conceal. "My elder brother inherited the manor along with my wardship and I don't blame him for anything." She was shaking her head slowly and looking off into the middle distance while everyone waited for her to tell them what it was she didn't blame him for. "I was raised alongside my nephews and they were more like brothers to me than my brother. But when I was old enough to be married, Alberic, that's my brother, was at a loss; he didn't have enough for a good dowry, although I was angry that he was withholding what was rightfully mine, I think he knew I didn't want to be married off, especially not to the kind of man who was willing to take the little we could afford." Wilfreda opened out her hands in a shrug. "And what else does one do with a burdensome sister?"

"He sent you into the Church?" Marian asked.

Wilfreda nodded. "Clementhorpe Priory. I was rebellious and miserable at first but after a while, I began to enjoy the routine and I liked the work in the herb gardens. I found I wasn't so miserable there and the rebellions gradually subsided. At least..." Wilfreda paused and looked at Robyn, there was something in her eyes; pleading? Robyn wasn't sure but Wilfreda went on cautiously. "It is forbidden for nuns or even novices to become too close to one another. Having a particular... friend is not possible..." she paused and looked around the table, then added hurriedly, "but you don't need to know the details. Let's just say, I was soon taught to pick locks and move around where I wanted to at night without the Abbess knowing... but as careful as we thought we were, we were discovered." Wilfreda breathed deeply as if the memory pained her. "We were sent our separate ways to serve penance. I was placed in Wix Priory, half-way across the country and with none of the comforts or leniency I had learned to rely upon."

Robyn caught Marian's eye and there was a look of guilt and pity that made Robyn wonder if Marian had been thinking the same thing that she had; wondering how they would feel being torn apart and sent to different ends of the country. It didn't bear thinking about.

"My good deeds did not carry with me to Wix," Wilfreda continued, "only news of my rebellions and somehow even my good work was looked on ill. I was given clerical work, the work I hated most and so paid little heed to completing it well. Wix was as small as Clementhorpe with just twelve of us, yet the Priory held the tenancy of many of the lands surrounding it and should have been as wealthy as an Abbey ten times its size. It was then that I first looked into the ledgers and noticed things I didn't even believe myself."

"What kind of things?" Robyn asked intrigued.

"Money was missing from the accounts, tithes, rents, donations. The money coming in didn't seem to match the costs. But in trying to correct my errors I only discovered more and more, until I was sure the errors carried back to before I was ever at the Priory. I took my discovery to a sister and I honestly believe, even now, that had she taken a moment to reassure me, I would have left it there."

"But she did not?" This time it was Marian who asked the question, leaning forward on her stool, hanging on Wilfreda's every word.

"No," Wilfreda turned to Marian, "she was furious. I thought she would blame me and make me go through all the old accounts to find and correct the problem."

"So, what happened?" Marian asked.

Wilfreda shrugged. "She wanted me to bury it and move on. That was their mistake then. They could have moved me to the gardens, the kitchens, the infirmary, by that point they could even have had me embroidering, anything to get away from those ledgers! But it was my penance." Wilfreda sighed. "I was utterly alone for long hours, week after week with nothing but piles of paper and the scratching of the quill as I kept up our ledgers. It wasn't just dull, it was..." she breathed hard as if searching for the word, "excruciatingly lonely."

"So how did you get out...?" Robyn pushed.

Wilfreda shook her head. "I was a determined little fool. As angry as I was, and as miserable as I was, I still had faith in people. That was where I went wrong." She laughed bitterly and looked down, picking at the bandages that bound her hands. "I didn't just keep the records they wanted me to. I made a new ledger, going back through the months before I had even been there. I logged everything. It went back years, but I made new records this time showing the errors and keeping a record of the amount missing. It was eye-watering. We used less to run the Alms-house, we could run a second infirmary and take in the sick from the town at no loss to us with the money that had gone missing. We could lower our tithes and rents for all our tenants and still not match the amount that wasn't being accounted for."

"Where was it going?" Robyn asked.

"That is where I was particularly foolish," Wilfreda answered shaking her head, "I should have seen that the one sister could never have been alone in the theft. There would have been nowhere for her to physically store the amount. There was enough to build a palace and I really believed that a single sister in a backwater abbey was keeping it hidden. I should have known. But I was a fool and I went open and honest with my findings to the prioress."

"I take it that didn't go well?" Robyn said.

"I can still remember the look she gave. I had never liked that woman. In my mind, she was far too firm. But I had been told she was fair." Wilfreda shook her head and a slight snarl appeared fleetingly across her lips. "In that one look, I knew. I knew she was as wicked and as selfish as she had always claimed I was. That was when I realised my mistake. Only when it was too late." She sighed deeply. "Even when she called in the bishop from St Osyth, I had a foolish hope I might explain myself but..." she shrugged, "when I saw him... when I saw his clothes alone, I knew where the money was going."

"He was the bishop whose men chased us?" Robyn asked, thinking back to the men who'd been stalking the land since the day she had met Wilfreda.

She nodded. "The Bishop of Hereford." Wilfreda looked at Robyn and disgust coloured her features. "He's built a palace; he lives like a king while claiming to loyally serve one. People starve in the streets and he uses gold meant for them to stuff his own coffers, buy the finest weaponry for his men, and even make copies of his dreadful book."

"And you know this for certain?" asked Marian, who was still cautious while Robyn was already imagining how she could rob this bishop of everything the greedy cleric had stolen.

"Oh, I'm certain," Wilfreda replied with almost a growl. "They should have killed me. It was the only way I would be silenced after that. It wasn't only the injustice of the theft, although that bit at me, it was the way they had treated me, so hard on my sins that hurt no one as they themselves committed sins that ruined lives." Wilfreda shook her head and bit her lip, Robyn could see the anger afresh coursing through the young woman's veins, she could see it because she felt it herself.

"So, what happened to you?" Robyn asked, wondering how she had managed to turn the tide on them and end up with a sack full of gold over a hundred miles from where she'd started, and a heavy price on her head.

"They ordered me to a hermitage to serve yet more penance. Alone on a windswept rock at the mercy of the waves and those who remembered to send supplies, although I knew that no one would remember and I was being sent there to die." Wilfreda shook her head. "They ought to have found some way to execute me, but" she laughed bitterly, "they have made their canon law so easy on themselves that they have little way to rid themselves of enemies from within."

"But you escaped?" Robyn asked.

Wilfreda nodded eagerly. "I didn't have many days, I thought of a thousand ways out of the mess I was in but only one that didn't rely on anyone else. I still had my tools with me, smuggled in my belongings and hidden in a crevice in the floor, I knew I could escape, but what then?" She looked around them. "It was the only choice open to me. I escaped my cell and broke into the treasury, then I loaded everything I could onto the donkey and ran." She sighed and looked down. "There was a guard at the main gates. There had never been a guard before, but of course, he was there on my account. I won his sword and injured him..." her voice trailed off but no one pushed, they were silent waiting for her to continue. When she did speak again her voice cracked, but she held herself steady. "He must be the man they say I murdered. Though I did not know until today that was the case." She was pale and her eyes drifted into the middle distance.

Robyn remembered hearing the news of Theobald's death. The shock and sickness that came over her. She remembered too, the moment she had injured him as he ran at her, his sword ready. She'd unleashed an arrow in a jolt of shock. He'd screamed then, pulling the arrow from his shoulder in a fierce rage and the blood poured from the wound staining his shirt. But she hadn't heard of his death until the next day and the sickness and guilt of it had coursed through her.

She would never forget it.

"I regret his death," Wilfreda continued, "but not my actions. After that, I just fled."

"Where were you heading?" Marian asked.

Wilfreda sighed and looked at her with a shrug. "I had a notion of going back to Clementhorpe. I managed to keep low and evade the search for some days as I made my way north, I was often given a bed for the night and food by those who wished to help, although I kept away from churches. It was only in Oakham, not too far south of here, that somehow the hue and cry went up, it must have been that damned poster you found. After that I decided to stick to the less travelled roads of the king's forest... and by the devil or the light, I ran into you." She looked at Robyn then. But her story was over, she had nothing to add. Now it was the turn of the others to make their voices heard.

There wasn't a sound.

"Here you all are." Alis, Merek's daughter, huffed up the stairs shattering the silence. "Are we to open for lunch or leaving the townsfolk to starve?"

Robyn glanced at the others then stood. "Alis, would you see to Wilfreda's wounds?" She indicated the young woman and although Alis narrowed her eyes, she nodded. "She has been riding all morning and they may be sore again," Robyn explained.

"Aye, all right," Alis said, beckoning Wilfreda with one hand and pointing to Merek with the other. "But mind you don't leave me alone to tend to customers."

"Aye, Aye," Merek nodded looking harried and pale.

Wilfreda stood and went to join Alis on the stairs, then turned to Robyn. "You're going to be deciding what to do with me aren't you?"

Robyn's stomach twisted, but she wasn't of a mood to lie. "Yes." She nodded.

19

THIEF LIKE ME

As soon as Wilfreda Gamwell had left down the stairs with Alis, Robyn turned to the others.

"I knew," Merek started, wiping his brow and leaning on the table, "I knew I did not like that one the moment she stalked in."

"Aye," Littlejohn nodded slowly, "she's not been honest for one moment since we met, that one." He leaned forward, plucking another morsel of food from his trencher and sighing deeply.

"She was polite enough," Marian added, "but she has far too much skill with a sword, more like an assassin than a sister."

"Aye." Littlejohn nodded slowly. "And those tools of a master thief she carries. Where did she find those?"

"A master thief?" Merek asked, his voice rising an octave, as he sat himself heavily on a stool. "Bless my barrels they'll burn all of Nottingham seeking her out!"

"So, am I to take it," Robyn asked standing over her friends as they sat cosily around the table discussing Wilfreda's fate, "That you are all against her?"

They turned to look at her, silent for a moment before Marian spoke. "Are you not?" she asked carefully.

"I'm not ready to condemn the woman," Robyn said flatly.

"She's a proven thief" Littlejohn pressed.

"And a liar," Merek added.

"Not to mention a murderer," Marian said.

"Not one of us has kept within the law," Robyn pointed out.

"Aye, but," Littlejohn glanced at the others, there was an awkwardness in his tone, "the sheriff and the Church are at her heels, there's no knowing what will come of it."

"If they find the woman is here," Merek shook his head, looking paler than ever, "it shall be my head for the noose." He clutched at his neck as though he could already feel the rope pulling at his throat.

"So, you would turn her in?" Robyn asked, her hands clenched into white-knuckled fists.

"We cannot keep her here!"

"She's been dishonest from the start," Marian added, "there is little reason to believe she is honest now."

"And what of you, giant?" She almost growled the question at Littlejohn, so tightly was her jaw clenched.

He shook his head with a slow shrug. "'Tis not my place to forgive her sins, but I still see malice in that one's look. She has a heart of stone, the hands of a thief, and the silver-tongue of a well-versed fox."

"Then what would you have us do?" Robyn snapped, her tone sharper than she had intended, but she struggled to hold back. Her friends said nothing and she pushed again. "Should we hand her over? Collect her reward and watch her hang? Is that what you wish?"

"Nay," Littlejohn said slowly, "but..." he didn't find the words to finish and spread his hands in a sign of defeat.

"We would be aiding a murderer, Robyn," Marian said.

Merek nodded. "Giving sanctuary to a murderer is as bad as doing the thing."

"Aye," Littlejohn sighed, looking to Merek, "that's true enough."

"But you're already aiding a murderer!" Robyn said, they turned to her and stared, "or have you all so soon forgotten that I was the one who killed the sheriff's own kin? It is by my hand that he lies dead." She couldn't prevent a crack on her voice and she looked to her boots in shame.

Marian touched her arm gently and her voice was soft. "That was in your own defence, Robyn."

She shrugged, breathing deeply to recapture her voice. "And what was so different in Wilfreda's tale?"

"But..." Merek stammered a protest but there were no words forthcoming.

Robyn looked to Merek then Littlejohn and each dropped their gaze from hers. "Is it because she is haughty? And proud? Is that what condemns her in your eyes?"

"She didn't tell us, Robyn." Marian was firmer than she expected, "That shows we cannot trust her."

"And should I confess my own sins to every stranger I meet on the highway?" She held Marian's gaze and her warm, blue eyes seemed to turn icy cold.

"We don't know the lass," Littlejohn pointed out, his tone was soft, but his suggestion showed a coldness in his heart, "she may keep worse hidden."

"So, it is because she is a stranger, is that it?" She pulled away from Marian moving to stand in the centre of the room and looked to Littlejohn. "Was I not a stranger to you, not more than a few weeks ago? And to you Merek?" Robyn took a deep breath and tightened her jaw pushing down a welling rage. *Were her friends so shallow? Just how lightly had she won their favour? What different turn of phrase or manner would have seen her abandoned by them rather than taken in? How easily could their backs turn even now?* "That woman is no stranger at all. She is no stranger to any of you because it is only by God's grace that her place and mine are not traded."

There was a long silence, finally broken by Marian. "And if that were the case, Robyn?" she spoke softly but with no less severity, "Do you honestly believe that if she were stood in your place, that her argument for clemency would be as passionate?"

Robyn didn't know. But there was a fury in the pit of her stomach that didn't care. It didn't matter what Wilfreda might do in her place. It only mattered what Robyn did now. She picked up the wanted poster that lay on the table between them. She stared at it for a moment and then balled it up in her fist and threw it in the fire. "If you are my friend, then you are hers. And if you are not..." she couldn't finish the sentence. She looked at them in turn. She wasn't their leader; she had no right to demand they follow her in any way.

In another life Robyn was the daughter of a baron, she could demand the loyalty of a dozen men and a hundred tenants. But now... it wasn't her place to command others against their will, and she didn't want it to be. "I know not one of you will stand with me on this, but I hope, at least, you will not stand in my way."

"Hear Hear!" The shout came with a banging of a stick hard against the floor and the four of them jumped and turned to Merek's mother.

Despite herself, Robyn let out a chuckle. "Then I have one friend, at least."

"Y'know I'm with you," Littlejohn said, "no matter what daftness you're thinking." He leaned forward and ruffled her hair as if she were a mucky lad ready for mischief.

"I'm with you always," Marian said, and her words lifted a weight Robyn hadn't realised was so heavy. "If you'll have me?"

"Of course," Robyn replied, returning the smile and feeling lighter than air.

"Well," Merek said, wringing his hands and looking at his most uncomfortable, "if I can help without getting a noose around my neck, then so be it."

"Good," Robyn said with a nod, "Because I need you most of all," she added, with a grin as she thought of a way to put a greedy churchman in his place without harming a hair on the head of a single innocent.

Merek stared with his mouth agape. No doubt wondering why the young outlaw felt a portly innkeeper was her most useful ally.

Robyn smiled at the innkeeper's bewilderment. "I have a plan to make the Bishop of Hereford pay for his excesses. Literally," she looked around at her three friends. "Are you in?" They glanced at one another then nodded in unison. "Good, now this is what we have to do-"

20

THE KING'S DEER

It was a warm afternoon in the first week of October when Robyn and her friends were once more deep in the heart of Sherwood Forest, just three short days after the outlaw's council in the back rooms of The Blue Boar.

Beside her was the ever-loyal Littlejohn, and, still in the gifted scarlet gown, though she now wore hose and had cut the gown almost to her knee, was Wilfreda Gamwell.

Lady Marian of Leaford, in a hodgepodge of fine hunting boots, ladies' hose, and an old, borrowed shepherd's tunic and hood, was preparing her hunting knife with the grim look of determination she always wore in readiness for an unpleasant task.

The deer had been felled quickly. A fine-looking buck that had never known his fate and would serve their ends well.

It had been a good long while since Robyn had been part of a hunt.

She loved the finery and pageantry of a royal chase; it had been a pure joy and a privilege to rove the countryside with the old King Henry. Her father had been at the head of the hunt alongside the king himself while she was often further back with the ladies. She was always torn between two desires. She was eager to be part of the 'real' chase out with the men, feeling the wind in her hair as her horse galloped over hill and dale in swift pursuit of a hart or buck. But she was often just as happy to be far behind away from the noise and the carnage and close to Marian, enjoying the warm sun and the chance to talk of nothing and everything the world presented them with.

Today the outlaw's hunt had been nothing like a king's chase.

Littlejohn had led them, scouring the woods for the trail and pursuing silently for miles. They were forced to stay low and hidden from sight, not just to stalk their prey but to keep alert for any of the sheriff's men that may be on patrol in the thousands of acres of royal woodland.

But now that the hunt was successful it was time for the next stage of her plan.

The deer had been gutted quickly and carried through the woods to the meeting point, where it was now hanging from a tree by the side of the road awaiting their expert butchery.

The others had listened to her plan with raised eyebrows and more than a few questions. They found the idea slightly mad. Merek, most of all, felt that it couldn't possibly go the way she wanted, but she had promised that she would make up any losses to his larder. He was dubious of this and pointed out that, should they be taken to the gallows, she would be unable to keep her promise.

But the only alternative they could offer was to leave Wilfreda Gamwell to her own poor luck and accept that none of them had a single coin to live on through the winter.

When it came to it, not one of Robyn's friends was truly cruel enough or fool enough for that.

So, they sat, stood, leaned on a tree and listened by the side of the main road to Clipstone House waiting for the bishop's retinue to pass. They'd paid off one of the sheriff's castle guards to learn of the bishop's movements and had needed little more than a good piece of meat and a quart of wine for his loyalty. But the longer they waited the more Robyn wondered if perhaps the hapless guard Bert wasn't so hapless after all and he had fed her with false news while she fed him with beef.

Wilfreda sighed. "This is pointless," she said, kicking at a pile of dark bronze leaves.

"This beast can hang 'til overmorrow, we can try more than once."

Robyn looked up at Littlejohn and shook her head with a sigh. "How many days will Merek be willing to close The Blue Boar?"

"Not more than one I'd wager," he said sadly.

"Well, it's not a complete loss," Marian added, "We have venison at least and that can sell-" She stopped at the sound of a crow. "Is that...?" she asked wide-eyed.

Robyn stood up straight and Wilfreda drew her knife. They listened. Sure enough, two more caws, clear on the cool afternoon air, rang out through the forest.

"That was Allan," Robyn said with a nod, recognising the signal they'd agreed with the young tavern minstrel, "Spread out."

"You do know this is madness, don't you Robyn?" Marian hissed, her eyes wide and her cheeks pale.

Robyn grinned, although nerves swelled in her belly. "Just mad enough to work," she replied.

The familiar sound of hooves and the scraping of wheels

on the hard, beaten road caught their attention and just a few moments later, the first horses in a procession rounded the bend in the road up ahead.

Littlejohn stood with his stave in the middle of the road, blocking the path of the riders as if he had not a care in the world, as he supervised his three assistants starting the careful task of butchering the meat.

The horses slowed. The first few men simply ignored Littlejohn, going around him and paying him no heed. The fine covered wagon that followed, however, had a little trouble and was forced almost into the ditch to avoid him.

At this, a plump head wearing a bishop's mitre appeared out between the curtains of the rear of the wagon as it passed.

"Ho, what goes?" the plump head demanded angrily, first looking toward the driver and then turning to see the giant Littlejohn beside the unmistakable sight of the king's deer hanging from the tree. "What's this?" he blinked cloudy eyes at them. "HALT!" he called out and the horses immediately stopped. "What's this?" he demanded again.

Littlejohn turned, as if noticing the procession of men, horses, and the expensive covered wagon for the first time. "Fine afternoon, Bishop," he said with a low bow.

"It may very well be a fine afternoon, but what the devil do you think *you* are doing with it?" He was leaning out of the wagon now, betraying spots of crimson as he peered toward the venison.

Littlejohn looked about, his eyebrows raised and his mouth agape in a startling rendition of a bemused man. Robyn looked away, sucking in her cheeks and concentrating on her delicate task in the hope of holding down the giggles.

"Why sire," replied Littlejohn, in his best mock Norman accent, "we are preparing our dinner!"

The man blinked; the deer carcass was no more than four feet from him, yet it was only now it seemed his eyes had cleared enough for his suspicions to be confirmed. "How dare you!"

"Well, no one else will prepare it for us," Littlejohn replied matter-of-factly, "will they, lads?" he said, turning to the three young women.

"Nay," they said in unison, as Robyn turned away from the exchange, her whole body shaking with suppressed laughter, made only worse when Marian gave her a look that could have withered a field of summer flowers.

"You know very well what I mean, this is the king's deer!"

"So it is!" Littlejohn said, as if he had never considered the fact before, "and don't we thank him for it, lads! Long live King Richard!"

"Long live King Richard!" Marian and Will echoed, and Robyn was certain she also heard the mechanical replies of some of the bishop's men alongside them.

"I will not stand for your cheek man." The bishop flung his legs over the back of the wagon and slid down, ignoring the filth as his silk slippers splattered into the mud. "Don't you have any idea who I am?"

Littlejohn turned to the bishop and seemed to consider him for a long moment before answering. "You're certainly a fat priest, of that there's no doubt, but you cannot be that greedy old Bishop of Hereford, who's hereabouts for I heard he was the devil's own rogue and you have been naught but virtue itself."

"How dare you!" The bishop squealed in a pitch Robyn would never have imagined a man of his stature could attain. In his desperation to approach Littlejohn, he staggered and almost fell to his knees. A manservant scuttled forward to lend his aid. "Off off," the bishop pushed the servant away even as he was prevented from falling on his face, "You come when you're called and not before." The man withdrew red-faced and low. "Now you," the bishop continued, eyeing Littlejohn and pointing a swollen finger toward his chest, "how would you like to spend a night in the cells and a morning on the gallows?"

Robyn's hand drifted to her bugle, was it time? She took a deep breath. Not one of the mounted guards was looking her way, they seemed bored and inattentive. There was plenty of time yet to play with the bishop, and now it was her turn to see if she could make the crimson of his cheeks match the crimson of his robes.

"Your grace!" she said, moving away from behind the deer and toward the bishop, even as Marian hissed at her to stop. "Have you been so poorly treated by my men you threaten us with murder?"

"Murder? How dare you, you upstart!" He turned his clouded eyes upon her, "Do you wish to join your friend in a noose?"

"I'd prefer my own noose," Robyn said with a wink to Littlejohn, "if one could be spared. However, I would also prefer a fair and proper hearing. For justice that is too swift is often no justice at all."

"This is the king's deer," the bishop pointed roughly to the carcass hanging from the tree.

"And we are the king's men, are we not? Long live King Richard!"

"Long live King Richard," came the reply, and this time Robyn was sure of it; at least half a dozen of the bishop's own men had joined the call. She clenched her jaw, swallowing the smile and forcing her face into a stern frown.

"Are there any other charges you are laying upon my friend here? Or can we go about our business today unthreatened by a lordling who wields his master's justice for no one's benefit but his own?"

"Charges!" the crimson bishop replied and she wondered if steam would start emitting from his ears. "Poaching the king's deer, and insulting the king's justice, these are charges enough to see you all hanged!" He looked around at them while his men remained eerily still, no doubt each of them knew the wrath they would face if they showed so much as an ounce of their own initiative.

"Insulting a bishop!" Robyn cried with a gasp, "I would never believe it, of my men."

"Stop your foolery, you can act as a witness yourself, for it was not said so long ago."

"Is this true?" Robyn wheeled around to face Littlejohn; the giant of a man hung his head in melodramatic shame.

"My lord," he replied, in the perfect imitation of a lowly villein about to be whipped by his young master, "I did call the man a fat priest."

"You called the Bishop of Hereford himself a fat priest?" Robyn repeated the insult loudly enough to ensure no one's ears had to strain for the words.

"Aye, my lord," Littlejohn repeated.

In the corner of her eye, Robyn could see one of the bishop's men shaking, as the pikestaff he held wobbled vigorously.

"Well." Robyn let out a deep sigh, shaking her head and turning sincerely to the bishop. He appeared to be a man so desperate for obedience and a type of justice that suited his own ends, that she thought he might purr in delight when he eyed the look of deep apology she gave him. "I am sorry to hear this, your grace..." she bowed low, her hand on her chest in mock sincerity.

"Well..." the bishop replied with such a long-contented drawl that she was almost certain that, had she left their conversation there, he may have been so pleased with himself he would have left them without further reproach.

"For, of course," Robyn added sharply, "you must be a fat priest, as Littlejohn here is an honest man and he would never say a false word, least of all to a bishop."

The mood broke in an instant.

The bishop's face returned to his crimson rage, and the man with the shaking pikestaff could no longer conceal the laughter that burst from him. He was not alone and the bishop's guards, as well as her friends, snorted and guffawed.

As the bishop turned back to his retinue, threatening each of them with the gallows, Robyn allowed her grin to slide into merriment and laughed alongside her friends.

"Swift justice is God's justice and I shall have you all strung up for your insubordination this minute, men!"

Now it was time.

Despite her laughter, Robyn knew the danger was acute. She fumbled for her bugle as the bishop's men tried to pull themselves together enough to prepare to hang the four poachers from the branches overhanging the road.

The moment the three short bursts from her bugle rang out across the forest, the bishop's covered wagon and his retinue were surrounded.

The men were startled, some of them gasped in horror. Robyn had endeavoured to make sure not one of the townsfolk could be recognised, and each of them wore a costume and mask from the recent Michaelmas play.

It wasn't the people of Nottingham who appeared out of the woods with bows and scythes and pitchforks, but the angels of God, the children of God and the fallen angel himself making the most of the fearsome antlered costume Littlejohn had been only too glad to contribute to the jest.

"What in God's name is this?" The bishop choked out his words, and Robyn was surprised to hear a note of fear upon his voice.

But she had to admit that with the closing of the day and the long shadows in the woods, the eerie sight of the players and townsfolk in masks was powerfully disconcerting. She was sure that even if the bishop's men had not been outnumbered three to one, they still may have surrendered to her.

"This," Robyn said, gleefully in control and stepping out in front of the wagon so that all the bishop's men who had so far only heard her voice might see her as she pulled back her hood, "is an invitation to dinner."

21

MERRY-MAKING

The Bishop of Hereford's litter and his retinue of recently disarmed men were led through the woods by the costumed rabble. They had left the wagon and horses behind, while four of the strongest men held the large bishop aloft on the wooden litter which had been pulled from inside the wagon and was now arranged with cushions and blankets. Impromptu music arose from those who'd managed to bring drums, flutes and lutes as well as their weapons and, as the party weaved their way through the trees and over the uneven ground, it was more of a grand procession than the kidnapping of a high official.

Littlejohn had selected an open area of woods not more than a mile from the road. Although it was less defensible than their previous camp it was far better suited to the number of people.

As the procession entered the clearing, Robyn beamed. No one had been idle in their absence.

A good fire had been set in the centre, and lanterns lay on the ground surrounding the perimeter or hung from branches, newly lit now that the early night of October was starting to fall. Furs were laid out on the ground and a few wooden stools had been brought in from The Blue Boar, these, along with several fallen tree trunks heaved into place, were acting as the setting for the festivities.

Merek and Alis, in the costumes and distorted masks of terrifying angels, rushed to pour drinks and prepare the spit. There would be no time to roast the venison whole but the choicest morsels would do well to be slow-cooked and would add to the feast already prepared.

Two trestle tables had been set up, one with the drinks including hot spiced wine and honey, with honey mead and half a dozen jugs brimming with good ale. The other table was heaving under the weight of all Merek's best recipes. There was makerouns; melted cheese and butter between sheets of melt-in-the-mouth pastry, pork pies with eggs and spices, and stewed chicken in a wine broth all freshly made and steaming hot. Next to these were the sweets; red gingerbread squares with cloves, baked pears, apple pudding, blackberry pie with cream, and Robyn's particular favourite, a sumptuous elderflower cheesecake.

Robyn turned to the bishop's litter, noticing the men who carried it made little attempt to halt the fierce and unsteady swinging. It swung left and right as they clambered over branches and around trees navigating the uneven path toward the clearing. She almost pitied the poor bishop who gripped both sides of the litter, as his cheeks lost their crimson and turned a sickly pale.

"Welcome, your grace, Bishop of Hereford, to Sherwood Forest and to the festivities held in your honour!" She knew this would gain his attention. Had he been able to speak through his nausea, she was certain he would have been muttering, swearing and cursing her name. Promising them all that he would not leave his litter so help him God, and they would have to drag him from it by the ears. But at her flattering words he was set down, his eyes widened at the glittering lamps and she was sure that, though he might not see the feast, he would certainly be able to smell it.

Robyn grinned.

"Wine all around!" she announced. Her own people cheered and poor Merek or Alis (for it was impossible to tell under the absurd costumes) was set upon. Goblets, tankards and cups were tossed across the clearing to cheering players, carpenters, apprentices and goat herds, and the two angels of ale dashed around with two jugs apiece.

Robyn noticed the bishop's men were standing around looking to one another unsure if they should be joining in or rounding people up. Her eyes fell on one in particular, a man she recognised from a few days before. Although no older than the others, his beard was white as a grandfather's and his hand rested on an empty scabbard at his belt as though his palms were itching to draw an absent sword. When his eyes fell upon her, she knew he recognised her from their fight in the woods, the day he had very nearly struck her down had it not been for Will's sudden appearance.

She nodded to him, in what she hoped he saw as a mark of acknowledgement and respect, then she turned to bark more orders. "When I say all around, I mean all around," she pointed out the bishop's men, "Littlejohn, get these fine men settled and get some wine into them immediately, the poor beggers have had a long day of service."

"Aye, my lord." Littlejohn grinned and bowed low as if he were the champion knight obeying orders from his king, and the guards followed him readily, most seeming genuinely delighted to be led to the furs and settled down with goblets and trenchers ready for their meal. Although, the bearded man gave one last withering look in Robyn's direction which sent a chill to her stomach.

"I hope you don't believe," the bishop, still sitting upon his litter, and narrowing his eyes at her in a way that made her wonder if his sight was clear enough for him to even make out her features, "that your impertinence will somehow be overlooked as a result of this absurd display!"

"Overlooked, your grace? Never!" Robyn placed a hand on her chest in mock offence and the bishop raised his eyebrows, before she added, "there is little joy to being impertinent if it is immediately overlooked."

Robyn heard a snort of laughter next to her and noticed a bright red hood and tunic. She had worried the bishop might recognise Will immediately but it seemed that either he was too short-sighted, or Will appeared so different in the low, scarlet hood rather than her usual nun's cowl that even her own prioress would have struggled to know who she was.

"I shall fetch you a drink, your grace, the long journey from Nottingham must have left you parched," she beckoned to Will who threw over a tankard.

"It seems I am at your mercy," the bishop replied, quiet as a mouse now his soldiers were merrymaking.

Robyn grinned as a costumed angel filled her tankard, then she kneeled down to the bishop, helping the old man find the drink and clasp it with both his swollen hands. "'Tis a fine ale, your grace, I'm sure a churchman such as yourself would not wish for anything richer."

"Well, I-"

At that moment, the tavern minstrel, Allan, struck a few

notes upon his lute. He was a narrow young lad who usually wore a fine, blue tunic with mock gold thread, but today he was adorned in the green, woollen fig leaves of Adam, the first man, with a painted eye mask covering the upper half of his face so his mouth remained unobscured. The chattering slowly simmered down as Allan plucked at the strings, and when he was sure he had everyone's rapt attention, he began his song of lovers and rivals, knights and witches, spells, swords and betrayals.

The lad had a gentle, smooth voice, and even the bishop was held in rapt attention. It was only once this first song was over that the feasting began, the cakes and pies were passed around, and the first slices of veal were enjoyed.

Robyn made sure that the bishop's trencher was never empty, nor was his tankard and that he had his share of pies and pastries. As the evening wore on, she even saw him swaying to the music and his scowl had converted to a lopsided grin. Meanwhile his soldiers had shed half their armour and danced merrily. The wine flowed along with the music and the laughter.

It was like the Michaelmas all over again, only this time there was one significant difference. Robyn navigated through the merrymakers, to the far side of the clearing, bowed and offered her hand to the lady Marian who was doing her best to ensure no one missed out on the honey cakes and gingerbread squares.

"Would you care for this dance, my lady?" she asked.

Marian's cheeks reddened. "In front of everyone?" she asked with a coy smile.

Robyn laughed. "It is usually better to dance to music," she replied.

With a nervous smile, Marian replaced the sweet things on the trestle table and took hold of Robyn's outstretched hand. As Robyn pulled her closer, she added, "But perhaps we can dance alone later."

"Robyn!" Marian shook her head with a smile and a laugh, and the dancing, eating, and drinking was, for just a few hours at least, all that concerned the pair.

22

A TOURNAMENT

The party was quieting, the musicians were tired, and the victuals were running low. Robyn knew it was drawing to a close and there was little left for them to do. She spotted Will in her bright scarlet outfit and made her way around the fire to her side.

The young woman was red-cheeked and merry, and Robyn found herself somewhat startled to see a grin across her lips rather than usual smirk as she sat and jested with Alis and the young minstrel, Allan.

"Will?" Robyn hissed, and she turned her bright green eyes to Robyn and her smile fell, she knew the time had come. "How much time do you need?"

"No more than an hour," Will replied, "But I shall need some strong arms with me, these are still a little weak." She raised her bandaged hands and Robyn nodded, glancing around the assembled townsfolk.

"Take the devil with you," she said, pointing out the Viking warrior of a man who'd taken on Littlejohn's mask and headdress. "and I think the Archangel Gabriel is the butcher's niece, she could wrestle a bear and I'd pity the bear." Robyn scanned around. "She must be hereabouts; you can't miss her for the wings."

Will nodded, solemnly. "And the bishop's men?"

"Merry enough to pose no threat."

"Then I shall be back within the hour," Will replied standing and placing her empty tankard down in her seat, "don't let them follow me."

Robyn nodded. "I shall keep them occupied," she promised.

Will nodded with a grim smile and Robyn watched as she hurried off, stopping to speak to the archangel and the devil who went off with her quite happily. She was putting a lot of trust into Wilfreda Gamwell, but she knew that Will was also putting a lot of trust into her. Now it was her job to get on with the next part of the plan. A distraction.

"A tournament!"

As soon as it was announced, her friends, as merry as they were, leapt into action, a hunting bow was brought forward, Robyn recognised it as Marian's, along with several arrows, all with different coloured ribbons, and a thin but sturdy reed, painted red, was brought forward to be the target with much ceremony by the young minstrel, Allan.

"Whomsoever hits closest to the target claims a prize!" She announced once the field was set.

Robyn was surprised when a few of the bishop's men not only stood to help, but joined the gaggle of eager archers taking part. Merek was the first to be persuaded to take a shot, and he blamed his mask for the fact that his arrow landed yards from the red reed target. But Alis, with a similar mask, fared far better and attributed her sheer luck to beginner's fortune; having never used a bow before.

The two bishop's men proved to be fair shots, although Robyn had hesitated for half a moment as she wavered over whether to hand a weapon to men who wouldn't have hesitated to follow their orders to kill her not more than a week before. But they were so set on the tournament that their eager faces didn't seem to comprehend that they could have felled her there and then with a yellow-ribboned arrow.

Littlejohn was one of the last to take his shot. She knew he was a fine archer; it had been his arrow that had so cleanly felled the buck that morning and she was prepared for him to win by a clear margin.

He took the bow, aiming high so the arrow might soar up and then fall back onto the reed target embedded into the earth. But before he took his shot, he dropped the bow to the ground, grabbed his stave and ran for the red reed.

It took Robyn a moment to comprehend that he was going to 'hit' the target with his stave. "Cheat!" she yelled, standing up and pointing as he swung at the reed. "Bring him down, men!" No sooner had she ordered it than half a dozen of the partygoers leapt at Littlejohn, including a few of the bishop's men, while the crowd chanted 'cheat' and Allan and the other minstrels began banging drums and playing music to assist the chase.

He was finally brought down by two angels and Eve, tackling him by the knees, and he was led back to Robyn shamefaced, as the reed target he'd attacked was righted. At least he *would* have been shamefaced had the man been able to wipe the grin from his lips.

"What say you? Braggart?" Robyn demanded as Littlejohn was harried to his knees. "Thou art a cheat and have been witnessed a cheat!"

"Confession!" he bellowed, through his laughter, "I confess to my crimes and ask for naught but the lord's forgiveness!"

All eyes turned to the bishop. "The man repents, your

grace, is he forgiven?" Robyn asked, leaning over the bishop who appeared as red-cheeked and merry as any other.

The bishop sucked in his cheeks, although Robyn thought she might have detected a trace of laughter at his lips. "All who repent are forgiven." He made the sign of the cross and Robyn wondered if the man would be so benevolent when he woke in the morning.

"Praise the Lord!" Littlejohn exclaimed, leaping to his feet.

"Are there any others who wish to take part?" Robyn looked around the faces, there were not many archers amongst them, even the bishop's men were likely more used to the crossbow than a hunting bow. She looked at Marian. "And you? Would you take part in the match, sweet lady?"

"Clorinda," Marian cut in, a sly smile across her lips.

"Clorinda?" Robyn replied with a laugh in her throat.

"Yes, Robyn Hood, sweet lordling of Sherwood Forest," she stood, dusting her hands and taking the bow from Robyn, "Clorinda, Queen of the Shepherdesses, is at your service." She curtsied and Robyn laughed.

"I didn't know that Shepherdesses had a queen."

"Well, of course they do," Marian replied, "for how else could they manage their flock? It would be chaos, Robyn." She briskly scooted Robyn out of the way and turned toward the target.

Robyn noticed the way Marian's hand brushed the stray hairs from her face as she readied her stance and nocked an arrow. Robyn suppressed an overwhelming urge to startle her, and instead stepped back and let Marian take a shot unhindered for once.

Marian paused for a long moment, holding steady, then angled the bow up toward the tree line, took a deep breath and released.

A soft thud told them it had landed, and Robyn rushed forward, grinning as she saw Marian's arrow pressed up against the red reed. There was not a finger's width between them and even Allan's good shot was a few inches distance.

"We have a winner!" Robyn announced, reaching out and indicating Marian.

"Surely not?" Marian replied, with raised eyebrows.

Robyn was confused, she turned back to the reed to confirm what she had seen, but sure enough the arrow had struck true. "You are-"

"But not everyone has had their try." Marian was holding out the bow to Robyn, who stared at it with mild distaste and shook her head.

"Take your turn, Rob," Littlejohn shouted.

"We've yet to see this famed skill of yours," it was Alis' voice from under an angel mask.

But Robyn shook her head. "No, no, my friends, I no longer have my own bow."

"You and that ruddy bow!" Merek shouted, "It will be with you in good time."

"Use the other bow," Littlejohn shouted, raising his goblet as he sat cross-legged and merry amongst his new friends in the bishop's retinue.

"Aye, use the other bow," echoed one of the bishop's guards, Robyn wasn't sure which, "use the other bow," the man stood, turning to his companions encouraging them to do the same and a great chant began.

"Use the other bow! Use the other bow!"

Robyn was red-faced with the attention as the minstrels took up the chant and began to beat drums, blow whistles and sing 'use the other bow' to merry tune. She knew there was no getting away from it.

"Friends!" she shouted, through laughter and easing

them to calm with her arms, "friends," she reached out and took the proffered bow from Marian and waved it to rapturous applause. "I shall shoot."

She laughed as everyone cheered. Marian tossed her an arrow with a blue ribbon and took a seat on one of the furs with the eager smile of someone who knows they have posed an unbeatable challenge.

The crowd grew quiet, whispering to one another to shush as Robyn focused on the little red reed sticking up from the ground in the dark of the forest. She nocked an arrow.

She smiled to herself. It felt like a lifetime ago that she had last played this game with Marian. One would outdo the other and then the first would practice their skill in secret to outdo the second on the next trip roving into the countryside. There was no malice in their competition. There was always gentle teasing, of course. But there was always too, a genuine admiration for the winner. And although she was always impressed with Marian's skill, Robyn was happiest when those beautiful blue eyes looked up to her with the adoration of someone who is proud of their dearest friend.

The fire crackled. A strong wind shook the trees high above them and melted to a soft breeze lower in the forest. Even with only the firelight, the conditions were perfect.

Robyn breathed deeply.

The reed was twenty yards ahead, Marian's arrow pressed into the ground next to it with nary a hair's breadth between them.

Robyn had made a similar impossible shot once before.

When all had seemed lost in the Nottingham tournament. When Theobald, nephew to the sheriff, had split the peg and even the officials had taken his win for granted, she had steadied her nerves and fired. Splitting the very arrow that split the peg.

It had been a wonderful moment.

But was it a fluke?

The air was thick with expectation. Robyn knew all eyes were upon her. But there was only one set of eyes that she cared about.

With a last glance to get her bearings, Robyn pointed her arrow high, held her breath and released.

It took a moment to see what had become of her shot. But the jubilant cheers of an over merry crowd conveyed her win before she could comprehend it.

Marian's arrow was stuck fast, but between her arrow and the reed, Robyn's own arrow had found its target. Pushing the red reed aside and pressing up against Marian's shot, the arrows had landed like two lovers embracing.

Marian laughed and shook her head. "And what do you win, oh Queen of the bow?"

As the music played and the dancing erupted, Robyn looked to Marian. "How about a kiss from the Queen of Shepherdesses?"

Marian smiled and raised an eyebrow. "And you think the queen would give out her kisses so freely?"

"Perhaps," Robyn answered in a half-whisper, "once the audience has gone?"

"Perhaps, then," Marian agreed.

Robyn opened her mouth to reply, but in that instant, she noticed the distinctive bright red of her returning friend. Robyn nodded toward her and when Will gave her a confident nod in return, Robyn grinned and raised her voice for the whole forest to hear. "And now it is time, your grace, alas for the festivities to come to an end."

23

CALL IN THE RECKONING

The bishop, red-cheeked and merry after a long evening of good food, good service, good entertainment and good friends, appeared almost dejected that his captivity was finally over.

"Well," he said, rising from his chair of furs and logs, and onto his swollen ankles, "I suppose you braggarts mean to leave us here, in the middle of the wood, lost in the dark while you disappear into the night?" His previous discontent was clearly returning.

"Not at all, your grace," Robyn replied, bowing low and graciously, "my men shall guide you and your company back to your wagon, where you may return to your previous journey. No doubt you shall all make it to the King's House at Clipstone no worse for wear and having had a good feast among friends."

"Hear hear!" someone in the crowd re-joined. It was nearly impossible to tell from whom the cheer came, but it was repeated by even the bishop's own men, red-cheeked, well-fed, and delighted at their unexpected feast.

"Right," the bishop was momentarily deflated and lost,

"well then, boy," he waggled a swollen finger vaguely in the direction of Robyn, "you make sure you keep out of trouble."

Littlejohn guffawed at this and Robyn couldn't hold back her own laugh. "Yes, your grace," she promised, "if trouble keeps away from me, then I shall keep away from trouble."

She heard a sharp, dry laugh from behind and turned to see Marian, shaking her head. Robyn managed a shrug of wide-eyed innocence before a grin emerged.

Even the best and strongest of the bishop's men took their time to gather themselves. She noticed Merek and Alis pressing a few sweet treats and bottles into grateful hands. Most of the townsfolk were to head back to the road with the procession and then head home along the road to Nottingham, while the bishop went on to Clipstone.

Although, from their merriment, Robyn wondered if perhaps they had pushed the wine onto the guardsmen a little too well. She wasn't sure if many of them could even mount a horse let alone keep to the direct road to Clipstone House. They might wander the woods until they fell down, stone asleep.

A torchlit procession of locals readied themselves, making use of the scattered lanterns still burning. Robyn whispered to Littlejohn to change plans and at the sight of the wobbling guardsmen he agreed, and it was locals rather than the bishop's men who heaved the litter from the ground and carried the bishop, who was far merrier than he had been when he entered the clearing, not more than a few hours before.

I wonder how merry he shall be on the morrow, Robyn thought to herself with a sly smile.

Finally, they set off, many were singing a bawdy tavern

song without a care in the world that one of the leading men of the Church was amongst them. The lanterns and singing trailed off through the forest, and Robyn was a little sad that the merry feast was at an end.

"Well done," Marian was at her side and reached out to gently rub her back.

Robyn nodded with a grin. "Let's see just how well we've done." She turned to the few who were left at the campsite. The minstrels had remained behind, as had Merek and Alis, but it was Will that she was looking for.

"Ought we not wait for Littlejohn to return?" Marian asked.

"He shall be back soon enough," Robyn replied, knowing that wasn't quite what Marian had meant, but she was too eager to see the spoils. Wilfreda was leaning against one of the trestle tables talking to the now unmasked Alis as she cleared the few plates and jugs that would be returning with them to The Blue Boar.

"How did it go?" Robyn asked eagerly, interrupting their conversation.

Will looked at her with a single raised eyebrow and a satisfied smirk. "It wasn't easy," she replied, and despite herself, Robyn's stomach tightened. "These things are still useless," she held up two bandaged hands, and the innkeeper's daughter clucked.

"They ought to be healing by now," Alis put down the jug she was holding and reached out to take one of Will's hands in her own.

"They are much better," Will protested, pulling away from the fussing nurse.

"Well," Alis replied, though there was disapproval in her voice, "you come and see me if they are causin' you mischief."

"I shall."

"But did you manage it?" Robyn asked, now desperate to know if the whole scheme had been worth the effort.

"See for yourself," Will stepped aside and, tucked under the trestle table behind her, were three heaving saddlebags.

Robyn grinned at her friend with an impressed shake of the head and a whistle as the excitement seared through her. She almost didn't want to look inside in case their haul didn't live up to her hopes. But she squatted down and pulled out one of the heavy saddlebags, took a deep breath, and opened it.

Gold.

"Bring me a lantern would you?" She said the words to no one in particular but almost immediately a light was at her shoulder and glinting upon the precious metal.

"My word," Marian whispered.

"I never seen the likes," Alis said.

"I took everything except his blasted books," Will said with a grin that almost didn't suit her usually sharp features.

Robyn plunged her hand into the bag, the coins were cold against her skin and she could feel their weight even as she plunged her hand down. She half expected the bag to be stuffed with something else at the bottom, but it was coins all the way down. The same ones she had seen in Wilfreda's belongings back when she had been claiming to be Sister Mary, only now there was double, if not triple the amount. Plus a few silver coins she was sure were the very ones stolen from her own chest.

Robyn hauled out the next bag and the next. All stuffed with buttery, gold coins and a few scattered silvers.

There was more than enough to pay the winter rents of every citizen of Nottingham and beyond, even if they were doubled. There might even be enough to bribe a few officials and buy back the family estate of Loxley, though she doubted she could last long at home unless she cleared her name.

"Am I the only one who ever does anything?" Merek barked from the far side of the clearing.

Robyn jumped up forgetting her fantasies and beckoned Merek over. "I promised I'd make it worth your time."

There was a sharp intake of breath as he laid his eyes on the open saddlebags. "I never seen the likes," he whispered, his tone the mirror of his daughter's.

"This one's yours," she said, heaving one of the bags along the ground toward him.

"All of it?" Merek and Will said in unison.

Robyn laughed. "Take what you need and make sure all who were here tonight get their share. Then if there is enough left, make sure it goes to those who need it. We shall hide the rest."

"There'll be enough," Merek said, not taking his eyes from the gold.

"Oh, and Merek?"

"Aye?" he said, tearing his eyes away from the coins for a moment.

"Buy your mother something nice."

He laughed. "Aye, we can do that." He nodded heartily and clapped his hands together with a merry grin that looked set to stay on his features for days to come. "Right, who amongst you is sober enough to load up?"

Will put up her bandaged hands by way of an excuse but Robyn, Marian, Alis and Allan the minstrel, as well as the few remaining travelling players who'd loaned the costumes and would now be paid well for their troubles, were all ready and eager to help. Merek's wagon was piled high with trestle tables, empty flagons, barrels, plates, crates, and finally, his hearty share of the bishop's treasure.

It was a long ride back to Nottingham, and although Robyn begged them to stay, Merek insisted that he and Alis get back before sunrise, lest his mother never forgive him for closing The Blue Boar two days in a row.

Littlejohn returned just in time to wave them off and assured Robyn that the bishop and his men had journeyed on to Clipstone House quite merrily. Even if they discovered their loss before the morning, they wouldn't find their way back to their temporary camp in the dark. Meanwhile, the torchlit procession had headed off in the other direction back home to Nottingham and would no doubt already be able to see the gates of the town.

Once Merek and Alis had gone, and their new treasure hoard had been safely concealed until morning, the gang of outlaws and players settled themselves back around the fire. There was still a little ale left and a few of the gingerbread squares remained untouched, though more than one of the partygoers picked out the clove and threw it into the fire. Allan, the young minstrel from The Blue Boar, plucked at the strings of his lute while his new friends sat around the low flames of the bonfire and recounted the evening's events.

"It could have gone so wrong, Robyn." Marian leaned her head upon Robyn's shoulder and clasped her arm looking up at her with bright blue eyes that sparkled in the firelight.

Robyn nodded with a laugh. "I thought for sure the bishop would order a charge when Littlejohn called him 'fat'."

Littlejohn laughed heartily. "'Fat' weren't the insult,

Rabbit," he said, slapping his own round belly with both hands, "it were 'priest'."

Robyn laughed and wondered how crimson the bishop would have grown if Littlejohn had admitted that to him.

"I don't know why we didn't kill them all while we had the chance," Will said, with a note of bitterness on her voice, silencing everyone. She poked at the embers with the tip of her sword.

"You don't mean that," Robyn stated flatly, but from the sharp look Will gave her she wasn't completely certain, "besides, I doubt so many of the townsfolk would have come if they had thought it would have meant a fight to the death rather than a feast."

"We could have poisoned them."

"With Merek's food, we may well have done," said Littlejohn, following up with a deep belch that sounded as though the caverns of hell had opened and released a beast into the night.

Robyn laughed. "Well, we won the gold and no one was hurt, so I for one, am happy this is all over."

"I think you did well," Marian beamed up at her and stifled a yawn. If Robyn had achieved only Marian's admiration it would have been worth all the trouble of the night and more.

"Come along," Robyn said heaving herself to her feet, "let's find you somewhere to sleep." They took hands, and Robyn led Marian to a bedroll of warm furs and soft cushions still laid out. Marian set herself down and by the time Robyn had fetched a blanket, Marian was sound asleep and breathing slowly and deeply.

Robyn smiled and settled herself in beside her. She lay a gentle kiss on Marian's cheek and wondered how she could ever have believed it was a good plan to keep away from her.

She snuggled in, scooping the young woman into her arms and finally feeling the exhaustion of the day weigh upon her bones.

In no time at all, she fell into a happy sleep. Certain that the day could not have gone any better.

24

FOOL ME TWICE

The air was icy on her cheeks, but the warmth of Marian's back hugged up against her chest kept Robyn dozing far longer than usual. The sun was awake and piercing through the trees before she managed to open her eyes. Starlings were gathering to chatter in the boughs above the campsite, and a few dark brown leaves had scattered on the sleepers during the night.

A gently nagging headache was pressing on Robyn's forehead and, as much as she wanted to stay wrapped in furs and blankets, the thought of a pitcher filled with fresh water from the river kept pulling her from her gentle dozing.

Robyn rolled onto her back and looked across to see if anyone else was awake enough to send. The players were still there. Their costumes and masks piled high on their wagon. She wondered briefly if they would head back to Nottingham or move on somewhere else for the winter season, but they were all far too deep in slumber to send on an errand.

Littlejohn was still laying on his back, much as he had

been while they had enjoyed the last few sweet treats of the night, only now he was letting out the occasional rumbling snore.

It was no good. She would have to go fetch the water herself.

Robyn sat up, extracting her arm from under Marian and tucking the blanket back around her. Then she stood and stretched, looking around for a pitcher she could take to the river.

She paused and looked around again.

The players were all there. Allan the Minstrel among them. Littlejohn. Marian.

But there was no sign of Will.

The scarlet tunic was unmistakable. Even if she was buried under blankets, her raven black hair was easy enough to spot.

Robyn spun around, her eyes picking carefully over everything in the camp. The wagon ready to go. The bodies of the players sleeping around the dying embers of the large fire. The few furs and rugs still laid out, scattered pitchers and trenchers missed in the clean-up the night before.

But there was no Wilfreda Gamwell.

And worse; there were no saddlebags filled with the bishop's gold.

Robyn grabbed her sword. Will had fooled her once, she wasn't about to let that damned traitor get away with fooling her twice.

She took off, darting through the woods. There was no way she could pick out Will's tracks from the dozens of other tracks made the night before. She would have to choose a direction and hope that was the one the thief had taken. She headed toward the King's Road and by the time she had covered the mile or so from the camp she was already struggling and thinking back to that pitcher of cool water she'd promised herself.

She paused, looking up and down the road.

Will had talked about returning to Clementhorpe, so she would have headed north to York. Robyn started up the road north, a stitch nagging at her side but after a few paces, she paused.

Will would need supplies, and she would need to get those from friends. She might trade in that donkey for a horse, or even pay a ferryman to take her along the Trent. And the absolute last thing she would do was risk everything by riding past Clipstone House.

Robyn turned.

She knew Will might have left too many hours ago for her to catch up, that the traitor might have gone in any of a hundred directions. Robyn knew she would have stood a better chance of finding her had she taken the time to wake her friends and begin a search party. But maybe, just maybe she had guessed right, and the Wilfreda Gamwell she thought she knew would admit defeat and hand back the gold.

As she hurried along the familiar road, she ran all the scenarios through her mind but refused to let herself even contemplate returning to her friends empty-handed. Suddenly, she realised she was running out of time; when she rounded the next bend in the road, she would see the town of Nottingham sprawled out before her. There would be no way of knowing where Will was or even if Will was within those walls.

But as she took the turn, she stopped dead.

"Halt!" she shouted, as her mind managed to catch up with what she was seeing.

It had only been a few days, but she'd already forgotten

what Will looked like in her Benedictine habit, so much so that she might have darted past the nun and her donkey, loaded up with two heavy saddlebags, before realising.

But it was Wilfreda Gamwell, there was no doubt, and at her words, the nun stumbled, then turned slowly to face her. "You must have a nose like a bloodhound."

"I do when it comes to my gold," Robyn replied, panting, "What exactly is it you think you are doing?"

Will threw up her hands and laughed. "What does it look like?"

"I think," Robyn edged closer, she didn't want this to come to a fight but if she had to hurt Will in order to save the gold, then she would, "you're stealing from your friends."

"I don't have any friends," Will snarled her words then smirked, "and from the look of it, neither do you."

Robyn shook her head. "That's where you're wrong, my friends are loyal to me, loyal to the death and I am loyal to them. To all of them." She took a step closer, even now she didn't want to give up on her. "Even you."

Will laughed. "There's no such thing as loyalty," she marched closer and, despite herself, Robyn took a step back as she saw the wild look in Wilfreda's eyes. "I know you," she snarled, "I know your type, and I know you will betray me the first chance you get. So, I intend to get there first."

"You're wrong!" Robyn stammered in shock. "I would never-"

Will shook her head, backing away again toward the donkey. "You're not worth the risk."

But Robyn called after her. "I took the risk with you."

Will paused. She turned to look back at Robyn and there was something behind those green eyes that Robyn couldn't place. Was it sorrow? Pity? Regret? "And look where you ended up," she said finally.

But Robyn shook her head, she didn't want to give up on her, she was still so sure that Will wasn't beyond redemption. "Just come back to camp."

"Don't you get it?" Will snapped, throwing her hands up. "I am not coming back. I am not your friend. I am taking my God-cursed money and I am heading out on my own!" Will was shouting so loudly that Robyn was sure the people of Nottingham could hear every word and would wander over to see the commotion for themselves.

But Robyn didn't feel angry. She just felt an overwhelming sadness. "Good people will go hungry without that money."

"Good people go hungry every day, Robyn." Will spread out her arms as if the evidence of her words was all around her. "No one looks out for us so we have to look out for ourselves."

But Robyn shook her head again. "You don't believe that."

"You're naive," Will replied and there was a hint of disgust in the snarl that curled at her lip. She turned away and retrieved the donkey's bridle.

But Robyn couldn't let her just walk away like that. She drew her sword but held her ground. "I can't let you take that gold."

Will glanced back, then paused when she saw the sword. "You'd kill me for it?" There was pure disbelief in her tone.

Robyn squared her shoulders; this wasn't how it was supposed to go. "Whatever it takes to stop you."

But Will laughed and carried on walking away with Robyn's gold.

"I mean it." Robyn started after her, she didn't want this to be happening, but she couldn't see a way out of it now.

Will didn't bother to turn to her again, she simply shook her head. "You won't fight me, Robyn. Not without your giant here to save you."

Robyn clenched her fists, if Will thought she needed to be saved by the others then she was only too happy to prove her wrong. "This is between you and me, Gamwell. No one else has to get hurt."

"Then you are even more of a fool than I thought." Will halted, turning to her donkey and drawing two swords from the packs.

"Your hands-" Robyn stammered.

"Are better than I claimed last night, yes." As if to prove her point she swirled the blades and took up a stance poised and ready. "Last chance to run, Rabbit."

On hearing the nickname Littlejohn had given her, Robyn snapped. She charged forward and, holding her sword two-handed, she brought it down with a hard clang. But Will held up both her swords in her defence.

Robyn had to leap back quickly to avoid a kick and barely kept up with the wild striking of two swords against one as Will beat her back step by step until she stumbled and fell backwards.

"You're no match for me, Robyn."

Laying on the ground facing down two swords, she almost wanted to agree. But as she slowly got back to her feet without Will moving an inch to stop her, she wondered if the thief was weakening in her resolve. "I'm not leaving," Robyn said, although she wasn't sure how long her bravery would last.

"I don't want to hurt you," Will said, and Robyn believed her.

"Then give me back my gold."

Suddenly, Will launched a whirlwind of strikes. Left, right, left, right, until Robyn could barely keep up with the blows. She dropped her guard and Will hit her hard with a left hook bolstered by the sword handle. Robyn tumbled to the ground, shocked and seeing stars.

"Just because I don't want to hurt you," Will said, "doesn't mean I won't."

Shaking her senses back into herself, Robyn clambered to her feet. Blinking to retrieve her sight. She wobbled slightly, the pain in her head was so intense it was almost numb.

"You should have stayed down," Will warned, and there seemed to be a genuine concern in her voice.

But Robyn gritted her teeth. She could taste blood. "You're not taking my gold."

Will sighed and took up her defensive stance with a shake of the head. "I'm not leaving without it."

Exhausted and bruised, Robyn made a dash to grab the saddlebags. But Will's sword came down in her path. She beat it away with a parry, but there was another, and another and no matter how many times she parried her away, Will was ready with a counterattack and Robyn's sword arm was burning with exertion.

Then suddenly, Will made her move. Robyn's sword was snapped from her hand before she saw the blow. As she watched the arc of the sword flying up over the road and into the bushes beyond, Will's fist slammed hard into her jaw and the next thing she saw was the road.

"Stay down this time," Will shouted. Robyn rolled onto her back and peered up at the two blades pointing to her throat.

"Make me," Robyn choked out the words, feeling heady

but certain, certain in her gut, that Will had no intention of killing her.

"You are a fool."

"I've been called that before," she couldn't help but laugh at that, but laughing hurt and her jaw ached. "Just give back the gold and end this," Robyn said, wiping away the blood that was trickling down her chin.

Will laughed then. "You'll have to kill me for it," she stepped back and lowered her swords, but Robyn noticed she didn't let down her guard, "and you're hardly in a position to do that."

"You'll have to kill me if you want to take it." Robyn didn't mean the words, she wanted to push Will but there was a flicker that crossed Will's eyes that made Robyn wonder if she had pushed her too far. But then Robyn clenched her jaw; after everything she had been through, after everything they had all been through, Robyn couldn't be left empty-handed. Not now there were people who needed her. People who relied on her.

"You shouldn't say that," Will replied, shaking her head, and backing away, "not if you don't mean it."

Will turned, making her way back to the donkey and Robyn saw her chance. Gathering her strength, she made one last leap, hoping to grab Will by the neck and pull her down.

The last thing she saw was the blunt end of Will's sword.

Then nothing.

25

CORNERED

Wilfreda Gamwell reached the front door of The Blue Boar Inn and hesitated.

Her hand trembled as she reached out to the handle. She knew the people inside could not possibly know of her treachery yet. She could get breakfast, food for her journey, and lay a false trail with Merek. She could even leave the damned donkey with him. She loved that stupid wretch of an animal and would hate to see him go to some black-hearted crook.

She glanced back at the creature munching at the hay in the feedbags usually taken by a guard's horse. The saddle-bags still weighed him down, and if this was where they parted then she would have to be the one to lug them down to the quay and onto a ferry.

She would manage. She could manage anything now that she had her fortune and her freedom.

So why couldn't she manage one last little deceit? Why couldn't she open the damned door?

Will sighed. Changing her mind. She should go somewhere she wasn't known. Somewhere she could slip in and away unremarked.

The door burst open. "Wilfreda?" It was Alis, the pretty tapster. She was carrying two buckets and grinned at Will. "I didn't expect you t'be up with the sun."

"I..." Will stood, watching blankly as Alis poured the buckets into the waiting troughs and the donkey started eagerly lapping at the freshwater.

"Get y'self inside. Pa will see to you, I'll not be long."

It was too late to leave now, that would only raise suspicions. She was being foolish. She shook her head trying to shake away the last few doubts about herself and marched into The Blue Boar. Merek was up and tending to the early patrons, and Will was surprised to see so many of them. There were four young men at one table eagerly finishing off their bowls of what looked like porridge while they talked and laughed raucously. Another table held two older men, more serious in their manner, taking in low tones over drinks, while another poor-looking creature hunched over the bar, her thin rags showing sharp bones underneath. Merek, red-eyed but no less cheerful for his lack of sleep, was grinning and filling the old woman's bowl to the brim with a hot porridge that smelled faintly of apples, cinnamon and honey.

"Welcome! Welcome!" Merek beamed at her when he caught her eye, "Sister Mary," he added with a wink, "come sit, come sit." He indicated a wooden stool and as soon as she took her place at the bar, a half-filled bowl was wafted under her nose and her stomach sang with its scent.

"I shouldn't-" she started.

"Nonsense, nonsense," Merek replied, slopping a second ladleful of the sweet breakfast into her bowl and handing her a spoon. She didn't know why she had resisted; she was damned hungry.

Merek leaned on the bar. "Now, if its Alis you're after, she's not long gone to the stable-"

"Yes-no-I saw her," Will said, between mouthfuls of hot, sweet porridge that reminded her how cold her journey had been, and how far she still had to go, "but I need to get back on the road-"

"Have you met Nora?" Merek asked, still beaming and indicating the hunched old woman.

For a brief and horrible moment, Will feared the woman would rip off her disguise and reveal herself to be none other than Robyn Hood, laying in wait to catch the traitor. The thought made her slightly sick and suddenly the porridge didn't taste quite so sweet. "No," Will replied weakly and nodded a greeting to the toothless old woman who waved at her with a dripping spoon.

"Poor old thing," Merek whispered, leaning over the bar conspiratorially, "Your one brought her in a week or so ago, she still likes to go back to her spot by the bridge for the night but least she gets hot meals, you know?"

"My 'one'?" Will asked, more than a little confused.

Merek stared at her for a moment. "Robyn Hood."

"Long live Robyn 'ood!" Old Nora cried waving a spoon.

"Long live Robyn Hood!" Came a cheer from behind her.

Will turned to the cheering men who bashed their empty bowls on the table and she wondered how many of them had been in disguise at the feast the night before.

"Quiet down lads!" Merek chuckled. "Don't overexcite yerself there, love," he warned as Nora splattered herself with a little breakfast and he was quick with a cloth wiping up the spillage on the countertop.

"But," Will stared at the wretch of an old woman, and whispered to Merek, "But why did Robyn bring her to you?"

Merek looked at Will with a frown. "Cause she needed looking after, that's why."

Will nodded mutely. Feeling queasier than ever and knowing for sure that she had made a mistake.

Her mistake had been to come to The Blue Boar. She was losing her resolve. Losing her certainty and when she had only herself to rely on, she always had to be certain.

"I have to go," she said, sliding unsteadily off the stool, "I have to go, somewhere..." she turned to leave, quite determined that she could find supplies elsewhere.

"Hold on!" Merek called after her. She was hesitant for a moment, thinking she should simply walk out, but the last thing she needed was to raise his suspicions. She had thought herself so clever to come here, to start her new life by taking all she could from these fools, but now she realised she should have kept her head down and walked right on past.

Will turned, forcing a beaming smile. "Yes?"

He dug around behind the counter and pulled out a long package wrapped and bound in leather cloth. "Your one's bow," he hissed as he handed it to her, "You can take it back up to her, right?"

Will slipped open the package, she could see even from a few inches of wood, that this was a fine and expensive noble's hunting bow. She could get good coin for it. She could almost feel Robyn's presence within it and suddenly she baulked at the idea. "No." She shook her head violently and pressed the bow back into Merek's hands. "I can't-I'm-I'm not going back that way. For a while." She forced a smile but she knew it was unconvincing and Merek held her gaze for a moment before relenting.

"Fair enough, fair enough." He secreted the bow back behind the bar, "But you'll stay for a drink at least?"

"No, I just, I came to say goodbye, because I'm going. I have to go." Will turned to the door. Suddenly, the tavern seemed too small, the ceiling seemed too low, and there seemed to be too many eyes upon her. But as she reached for the door it swung open and her stomach flipped as two town guards strode inside.

Will spun on her heel and looked to Merek. "Perhaps I will take that drink," she said, sliding into a table in the corner as the guards strode to the bar.

"Coming up, Sister," Merek said confidently, as he turned to the two guards, "and what can I get you, gentlemen?"

Will sat, frozen in fear. Her muscles were taut and her breathing shallow as the two guardsmen talked amiably to Merek. She recognised the Nottingham colours and prayed they didn't have her description. The door was only a few feet away but if she wanted to reach it, she would have to slide past them and at that moment, all her courage had abandoned her.

Merek's cat trotted over to her with a mew of familiarity, its black tail was bolt upright as it threw itself confidently at her leg, rubbing its whole body against her calf. It meowed at her in disdain and expectation and, even as her insides quivered in anxiety she leaned down, to gently pet the creature's head.

Her heart slowed slightly as her eyes remained fixed on the two men, unable to focus on what they were saying and only praying that Merek would seat them. If they would just find a table she could slip out. She could slip out and make a run for it. God's bones, she would even go back to Robyn if there was a saint who pitied her enough to help her escape.

For the first time that morning, her mind drifted back to the fight. *She'd given that foolish girl the chance to stay down. Why hadn't she stayed down?*

She knew Robyn's type. She had seen more than enough of them at the Priory. The type of mindless do-gooding noble who threw a few coins into the poor box to assuage their own guilt, then went to market and spent five times as much again on silks they would never wear or gloves they would forget they owned. Robyn wouldn't know what to do with all that gold. She'd given most of it to one man. What did Merek need with all that money?

She eyed him suspiciously, even as the innkeeper's trusting cat weaved its way around her legs. *Was Merek a danger to her? Would he sell her out? Was that why Robyn had given him so much? Was she buying his loyalty?*

The old woman, Nora, stumbled as she descended her wooden stool, "Thanks be to thee, Merek, and to you-know-who!" She tapped the side of her nose as she stumbled backwards and one of the guards rushed to catch her before she fell. He laughed as he helped her to the door while she berated him for his clumsiness. Once she'd left, he turned to his friend with a chuckle and an eye-rolling shake of his head. Then he caught sight of Will and his eyes narrowed.

Her stomach twisted and she cast her eyes down and away from his. As she did so, she realised what had alerted him. The accursed cat had pawed at her leg pulling up her habit to reveal the knee length scarlet tunic beneath. Frantically, she pushed the cat away and desperately tried to replace her skirts. But it was too late.

The guard loomed over her. "What kind of nun wears a fine, red gown under her habit?"

His friend took a step toward them. "One that ain't a nun, that's what."

The first one grabbed her bandaged hand. "And how did you get these wound's, eh? Prayin'?" He pulled her to her feet and she snapped her hand away making a bid for the door. It was too late now; they knew exactly who she was. She just had to make a run for it.

But as she dashed around a table one of the guards grabbed her waist pulling her backwards and throwing her down in her seat. He stared at her blinking as she held his own sword pointed to his stomach. His hand went to his empty sheath, puzzlement knotting his brows as she took the opportunity to land a heavy punch to his jaw. He was dazzled for a moment and the pain of the hit ricocheted up her arm already bruised from her first fight of the day.

Before she could dash past, the second guard was ready. His blade flashed into her path. But she had no time for pleasantries and it only took a counterstrike and a lunge before he was easily disarmed. Will ran for the door, knocking a stool from her path in her haste to retreat.

But she was too late.

Two more guards, swords already drawn, entered the tavern with grim faces made even grimmer when they saw who was causing the commotion.

Will lunged and parried, blocking their entry, but it was no good. One of the first guards slammed into her from behind, tackling her to the ground. She yelped in pain as heavy boots stomped her wounded hands, and her stolen weapon was snatched.

But even then, she fought.

Grabbing and kicking wildly, Will fought to the last as

the bruised and battered guards lost their patience and finally managed to drag the nun through the door, an armed guard to every wild and frantic limb.

The fight was finally over.

Wilfreda Gamwell had been caught.

26

MAGPIE

Robyn's head pounded and her throat was dry.
Her hands felt out for woollen blankets but there were only mud-caked leaves. She rolled onto her back and opened her eyes to the sky.

She wasn't in camp.

She was at the edge of the woods. Pulled into a ditch by the side of the road and what? Left for dead? No, if Will had wanted her dead, she would be.

A new morning mist coated the forest floor and promised winter ice and she could hear the distant bells of St Mary's above the rattling of carts and chatter of the market carried on the cool, still air.

Robyn breathed deeply, feeling a little sick as she remembered the fight. A hand went to her head to check for wounds but there was only dried mud caking her face and she didn't want to explore the bruises and bumps in too much detail.

Damn, she'd been so clod-headed.

She watched a lone robin flutter down to the forest floor and begin to pick through the leaf matter in earnest. Its black eyes darting here and there its little body hopping about.

She stared at it for a moment. "You wouldn't be fool enough to let a magpie into your nest would you, little friend?"

The robin looked up at her with its tiny little black eyes as if the creature were mulling over a reply. Then it seemed to sense something within her change before she even noticed it herself and the little bird fluttered up into the trees just as her stomach tightened.

She gripped fistfuls of earth in a rage that boiled over into a wordless roar of frustration.

But letting out the anger didn't make it go away. It swirled within her.

Why had Will been so cruel? Had she planned it from the start? No, she couldn't have done, how could she have known they would capture the bishop and take his money? Had she been lying all along, waiting for the opportune moment to strike?

No. Robyn didn't believe that either. Wilfreda Gamwell had been honest that day at The Blue Boar. Will had been vulnerable and open when she shared her story. Robyn had believed her then and believed her still.

Which meant Will was the fool. A selfish fool.

Robyn remembered, with sudden vibrant shame, her thirteen-year-old self. Old enough to know better. She had discovered a hoard of honey cakes in the pantry, thinking only of impressing Marian with her find, she took them all and they had run off together to the forest and eaten more than their stomachs could take.

When she returned to the manor, she discovered the cakes had been made for her sister's fifth birthday and the little afternoon banquet for the children had gone without Eleanor's favourite treat.

Her mother had said nothing. She had simply looked at Robyn, shaken her head and turned away. It was a silly little thing. But the shame of it still burned at her. If she had taken only two there would have been no harm.

If Will had taken only enough to get her to safety, Robyn would have given it gladly.

But Will took everything.

Was it spite? Had Robyn hurt her? Humiliated her in some way she didn't know?

No. She didn't think so. It was just like the stupid selfish actions of a greedy child and Robyn was surprised at how much she hated her for it.

Robyn stood up. She kicked the dirt where she had fallen and stared around the forest. She would have to find some way back.

She hadn't been out for long. She knew that. The morning was still young, which meant there was a chance her friends back at camp hadn't yet set out in all directions to search for her.

She crossed the road and started kicking around in the leaf litter, half in frustration and half in a vague attempt to find the sword she had lost. When she finally spied the thing lying in the dirt, Robyn had built up such a ball of rage in her stomach that she let it out by attacking the brambles. This resolved nothing and she ended up with a few more scratches and a torn sleeve. She didn't even feel better for it.

Finally, Robyn turned to head back to camp. Part of her hoped she would never find their camp again and she would be forced to wander the forest for the rest of her life, emerging only as an ancient old woman who could no longer recall the shame that led to her hermitage.

It had been her word that had urged her friends to trust in Will. Not one of them had trusted that duplicitous little stoat. But oh no, the grand and majestic Robyn was dispensing forgiveness as if she were the king of heaven.

I forgive you, and I forgive you... she thought, wielding her sword at no one. But forgiving lying thieves for their lying thievery does not convert them into angels of truth. They are still lying thieves.

Her brain must be made of mud. Why did Will have to take all the gold? For that matter why did the bishop have so much gold with him, why did he take so much from the Church when a man in his position could see the good it would do for people? Why did the sheriff put the rents and taxes up during a harvest when there were fewer men to help with the work?

But Robyn knew the answer. She knew it with a burning rage that turned her reluctant walk into a stomping march.

It was the same reason she had taken all the honey cakes meant for her sister's birthday.

Greed.

Dammit.

Robyn was sick of them all.

She marched into camp, barely even aware of how long the journey had taken her.

The others were barely awake but at Robyn's sudden crashing about, they started sitting up, clutching heads and groaning.

"Robyn?" Marian said, sitting on the edge of her bedroll with her arms clasped around her knees and her loose hair slightly askew from sleep. "What are you doing?"

Robyn didn't even look at her, she carried on grabbing

pots and knives and saddlebags and throwing them into a pile. "I'm going."

Even at Robyn's curt response, Marian didn't change her gentle tone. "Where are you going, Robyn?"

"York maybe. Or London. I'll go to Brittany. I'll join my mother in the countesses court." She was ramming someone else's leather jerkin into a saddlebag. "and... and if I'm turned away or I can't stand it then I'll just... I'll go on crusade."

"Crusade?" Marian replied, her tone a little more amused than surprised. "And will you be needing this pan on crusade? Or are we allowed to keep it?" she asked picking up a frying pan from the pile of random objects Robyn had thrown together.

Robyn snatched it back. "Even a fool has to eat," she tried forcing the pan into the overstuffed saddlebags, failed and threw the saddlebags over her shoulder and wielded her pan like a sword.

Her clothes were ruffled and torn, her hair was loose and dirty, and her face was caked in mud.

Marian laughed. "I'm sure you shall have no trouble retaking the holy land."

"Well, I'm no use here, am I?" her anger burst from her and Marian raised her eyebrows. "My father left me to care for Loxley and I lost it, within weeks. Weeks, Marian! My mother at least left me enough silver to reclaim it and I threw it all away at peasants and no doubt the sheriff will double their rents again in winter since they had so little trouble paying it this time. And then-then I win- no I steal; then I manage to steal the bishop's gold and..." The anger was crumbling into tears, her voice cracked and she clenched her jaw not wanting Marian to see her crumble.

Marian stood, all trace of her gentle mockery was gone;

she reached over to Robyn and ran her hands down her arms. Unable to take hold of Robyn's hands as they were fiercely clenched at the saddlebag and the frying pan, Marian took hold of Robyn's wrists and looked into her eyes. "Loxley wasn't lost. It was taken and you did everything you could. The fault wasn't with you-"

"But I-"

"Shh," Marian had a way of making a gentle whisper firm, "Your mother said nothing about buying back Loxley with that silver because she knew that was not an option, she told us to use it well. And you did. Perhaps the rents will go up. Perhaps they won't. But you cannot live out your life second-guessing the unintended consequences of your actions, you can only try to be kind, Robyn."

Robyn nodded, fighting her tears and unable to argue lest they escape.

"And as for stealing from the bishop, well it seems he stole that gold from the Church so I see no reason-"

"It's gone," Robyn spat her confession before her guilt could hide it any longer.

"What?"

"It's gone," she said again, "It's all gone." She let out a deep sigh at the relief of having unburdened herself of the news. "And so is Will Gamwell."

"Oh, Robyn." Marian shook her head gently and a hand reached up to Robyn's head, she wiped away some of the caked-on mud and Robyn winced as she did so. "Oh, Robyn," Marian whispered again, but her words were less of a reprimand and more of a consolation.

"Come with me," Robyn said.

"Come with you? On crusade? Robyn, I don't think-"

"To Brittany," suddenly she meant it, her path appeared so clear before her, "I could stand it with you there."

"How delightful for you."

"No, I mean it would be just like it always was, I can't go alone, I couldn't bear it."

"And how are we supposed to get there?"

It all made so much sense, it was all falling into place. "The same as my mother, we'll go to York and hire a ship."

"You get seasick."

"I won't with you there, please say you'll come?"

"How are we supposed to pay for this boat, Robyn, with your pan? How are we to get to York? It would take weeks to walk it, and besides..." she looked away.

"Besides what?"

Marian shrugged. "I don't want to leave." She looked up at Robyn with apology in her eyes. "Your father is strong, Robyn, he is off on crusade with the king, your mother is safe, far away from this in Brittany. My parents are vulnerable, my father is ill, my mother insists it's his fondness for lampreys, but I know she is not telling me everything. I know his conscience is tortured by opposing loyalties that shouldn't be in opposition. I feel... I feel something is on the brink here Robyn. Something very dark is happening in England and if we run away-"

"We'll be safe," Robyn finished for her.

"But what about everyone we leave behind?"

27

TRAITOR'S LUCK

"But what shall we tell them?" William paced. He breathed unsteadily and the blood rushed to his feet as his head swirled.

"Tell who?" Maud hissed. Her voice low, reminding him to keep his own panicked wailing to an absolute minimum.

"Everyone!" He nearly shouted, but changed his mind at the last moment, leaning toward his wife and hissing the word, even as he looked around for stray servants that may be hidden behind the tapestries.

Maud was calm. Too calm. He didn't know how she could remain so still, as ominous as black water in a bottomless lake. She looked at him for a long, hard moment, then continued to pack. She was emptying out the castle silverware from the heavy, oak sideboard and hiding it between clothes and blankets in their travelling trunk. It wasn't their silverware. It had been in the castle long before they had arrived and no doubt belonged to the predecessor. Briefly, William wondered if there was enough of it to buy their way out of trouble, but he knew if there was, Maud would already have done just that. And the panic enveloped him again. He felt sick. He sat down on one of the long benches running beside the grand tables in the castle hall, his head in his hands. How did it get this far?

"We will tell them we are going to Derby," Maud said, matter-of-factly, as if they were planning a day's ride out with a neighbour, and not double treason. *Was it double treason if you committed treason against traitors? Or were both crimes somehow annulled? Did it even matter, when he knew he would still be hung-drawn-and-quartered if the wrong side caught him out?* "We can leave Roger in charge," Maud continued, "he is a competent enough Bailiff, is he not?"

William shook his head firmly. He hadn't listened to a word Maud had said. He was thinking over their own plans in his mind and it seemed everything was the wrong way around. "We should head to York," he said, "not London," then he continued in a low whisper, "the prince only has to forgive a debt, but the king's justice must forgive us of treason, I see no other way, Maud, we are-"

"No, listen to me, William, we are useless to Prince John without money, but we have something to actually offer Chancellor Longchamp."

Even in the whirlwind of panic, she was calm, folding blankets and secreting silverware between the layers in the travelling trunk. The servants would think it was strange that they had packed themselves. He glanced around seeing someone hiding in every shadow. *Would they say something? Would they ask? How should he reply?*

"We will go to court," Maud continued, repeating the steps of her plan as calmly and firmly as a prayer, "we will tell them everything we know of the prince's intended betrayal, we will give them the name of every traitor we know, we will tell Chancellor Longchamp we could not come sooner as we had no proof-"

"We still have no proof!" William wailed, tossing his hands in the air, "You burn everything, woman! You even burn letters from my mother." His voice rose in his panic and he knew he had to hold it together better than he was managing. Why had he married a scheming woman? He ought to have married a farmer's daughter, a buxom, earthy woman who laughed and enjoyed Sundays. William didn't have the stomach for this level of duplicity.

"That woman's mad witterings are dangerous, William." Maud snapped, then took a deep breath. "But you are quite right, the king's court will doubt us. But we shall put them on their guard. Then, when Prince John begins making his move, they will see we were right and we shall be pulled into the inner circle," she rested a hand on his shoulder and looked down at him, "worry not, we will win through." A rare smile pulled at her lips.

"And if Prince John triumphs without us?"

The smile disappeared. Maud took a deep breath and stared at him for a long moment, then closed her eyes in defeat. "We deal with that when it arises."

He noticed she didn't say 'if'. A cold chill swept through his blood and he shivered. He wondered briefly why he had agreed to Maud's support of Prince John's plot, and then remembered he hadn't; Maud had pledged money in William's name without thinking to mention it to him. He should have been angry with her, but that would have been akin to being angry with a crow for being a crow. He shook his head and clutched his stomach, nervousness made him queasy and the dread of being caught for treason was more than enough to give him an endless supply of nerves.

Perhaps the Bishop of Hereford was right: maybe there

was still time for Maud to enter the Church and become a nun. The ridiculous thought almost lightened his mood.

The heavy door burst open startling the conspirators.

"M'lord," a dishevelled guard rushed in, his livery was torn at the shoulder, blood caked around his nose, and there was a prominent bruise emerging on his left cheek, "we've got her!"

William panicked. "Who?" he demanded, searching his mind. *Was there a witness? Did someone know of his treachery? What damnable turncoat had they captured?*

"Robyn Hood?" Maud asked, her eyes wide, expectant and a hopeful relief surged up in William, the outlaw, they had her. At least that particular nightmare was over.

"Nay," the guard shook his head and furrowed his brow. William's chest tightened again. "We ain't got *him*." The guard pointed behind him with his thumb. "We've got that Gamwell woman, the one the bishop were after."

His men had recaptured the one that got away. William breathed out the tightness in his chest, and the relief bubbled up once more. That, at least, would mark him in good stead in the eyes of King Richard's men. "Ah! Excellent news," William replied, although he knew he sounded less than jubilant.

"Has word been sent to the bishop?" Maud sounded strained, but the guard nodded and seemed as pleased with himself as he could be with his face still marked with his own blood.

"Aye, ma'am, the bailiff had a messenger sent soon as we were through the castle gates."

"Good," William replied with a nod, "that should put a smile on the man's face for once." At least business will take my mind off our imminent danger, he thought, then nodded to the guard as he stood. "I'm on my way." He gestured to the door. "Clean up and get back to your post."

The man nodded. "Aye, sire."

He retreated through the door, and William turned to his wife, breathing deeply and already feeling all the better for their ounce of good fortune. "This news will soothe the bishop, and that is a point in our favour, at least."

But Maud was pale, she leaned on the edge of the trunk filled to overflowing with stolen silver wrapped in innocuous soft furnishings. "Damn, that Gamwell woman," she whispered.

William hesitated. He knew he ought to hurry off and deal with the returned prisoner, but the sudden change in Maud stalled him. "Is everything all right?"

"This couldn't have happened at a worse time." She shook her head, then closed her eyes and clutched the bridge of her nose with her fingertips.

William was no closer to understanding. He didn't want to anger her or make his own dread worse but he had to know what worried her. "Maud," he asked, trying to keep his voice even, "is there something you need to tell me?"

"It is over, William." She stared at him, resolute, but he shook his head uncomprehendingly and she drew a long slow breath. "The prince's man is coming tomorrow to collect on our debt. We cannot pay and Prince John will not forgive this slight. We shall be fortunate if he lets you die quickly-"

William's mouth was dry. "Which is why we leave today."

"But everything has changed, has it not? You have a duty to fulfil." She leaned forward and her whisper became even lower. "Now we cannot leave Nottingham without arousing suspicion. The bishop will demand to know the reason for our hurry, he will discover our debt collector, and will have the proof of our treason he has no doubt been searching for."

William opened and closed his mouth then looked back at the door through which the guard had left as the slow realisation dawned on him. "We can't leave today," he said, now understanding fully why it was true, he looked back to Maud's pale face with a sickening resignation. "Because tomorrow, I must supervise an execution."

28

ARCHER'S RETURN

"Robyn!"

The familiar voice of Alis echoed through the wood startling the pair. Robyn wanted to push Marian further and uncover what dark prophecy she had foreseen in England but Marian pulled away and turned to the shout.

"We're over here!" she called. Even knowing the clearing well, it was difficult to find it again, and poor Alis was no tracker.

"Can ye take all the nonsense elsewhere?" Littlejohn groaned still half asleep and pulled himself to sit up just as Alis, red-faced and out of breath, finally came tumbling into the clearing. Robyn clenched her fists still tighter. She wasn't yet ready to deal with even more people to whom she would have to break the news of Will's duplicity. And her own foolishness.

"I ran..." Alis panted and pointed back toward the road, "all the way."

"What is it?" Marian asked, stepping toward her with a

gentle voice that held only the mildest hint of panic. "What's happened?"

Alis shook her head, getting her voice back as she waved around a long, leather-bound package. "I'm sorry," she panted and shared a look that Robyn could only describe as dread. "There were nothing we could do."

Now it was Robyn's turn to feel panic. *Had Will stolen from Merek as well?* She should have left that duplicitous fraud of a nun in gaol to rot. "It was Wilfreda wasn't it?" She asked already knowing the answer.

Alis nodded.

"What did she take?" Robyn's voice was a low growl but Alis stared at her.

"No," Alis replied, shaking her head, "she's the one what's been taken," she pointed behind her again as if the incident had taken place mere yards away, "By sheriff's men, there was too many of 'em. Pa just had to watch or else they'd 'av' taken him an' all."

Robyn stared at Alis, dumbfounded. Marian turned to Robyn and there was pity in her eyes. "I suppose it was bound to happen eventually," Marian said and although her words were cold, there was sympathy in her tone.

"Will's captured?" Littlejohn blinked and rubbed his temples; the poor man had got too much in the spirit of the feast the night before and now his head was no doubt paying for it.

"You'll fetch her back, won't you?" Alis looked at Robyn wide-eyed and hopeful and Robyn was surprised to see her eyes glistening with barely suppressed tears. "Just like before?"

Robyn opened her mouth but there were no words.

Marian stepped toward Alis and took one of the young

tapster's hands in her own, "Wilfreda..." she glanced back at Robyn before continuing, "is a thief."

Alis laughed, a short burst of confused disbelief. "I know that Lady Marian, I ain't daft."

It was time for Robyn to step in, it was time for Robyn to admit she had been played for a fool. "She stole from us, Alis. She took everything." Robyn turned to Littlejohn as he pulled himself to stand up, he was pale and red-eyed. "I don't know how much you overheard just now, old man," The feast had likely been the first time in a long while that Littlejohn had let his guard down, but he hadn't been the only one and couldn't be blamed for faults that lay with them all. "Will stole everything we'd claimed from the bishop and when I pursued her... well I didn't come out of it well..."

But Alis shook her head. "No, she never-"

"I'm afraid it's true," Marian interjected, "We ought not to have trusted her after all."

"I don't believe it of her," Alis looked at Robyn, there was pleading in her eyes and Robyn wished wholeheartedly that she could change the truth, "it's a misunderstanding is all."

Robyn shook her head, and anger welled up in her again at the memory. *How could Will betray them all? How could she make friends and then turn on them so easily?* "I didn't roll in this mud of my own accord!" Robyn snapped; she hadn't intended to, but the rage was too close to the surface to suppress. "There is a lump the size of a fist on my scalp, do you think I did that myself? That craven, deceitful, selfish..." Robyn screwed up her face as she tried to think of a suitable name and fell short, "scoundrel! She gained our sympathies, made us join her cause, then lay in wait until we were dead-asleep, likely even filled our cups and drank nothing herself, before making off in the night with all the coin we had," Robyn shook her head, fury bubbling through her, "then she fought me for it. She fought me!" She breathed out slowly, letting the last of the rage out with the last of her tale. "There is no mistaking it."

Alis held Robyn's gaze for a long moment. "But she wouldn't take this," she held out the leather-bound package and Robyn took it from her, "even when Pa asked her to, she refused. Is that the act of a thief?"

Robyn took the package. She knew exactly what it was but that didn't change the thrill of excitement as she loosened the leather bindings. It was new, brand new, not her broken bow mended, but a whole new bow crafted just for her. The bow maker was a master craftsman; she knew that as she released the lower limb from the bindings. It was beautifully crafted, with an intricate latticework of leaves carved into the woodwork, varnished, painted and smoothed. He must have used the weight and length of her broken bow to create a perfect match, then put his own artistic touch to it.

As she strung it, Robyn could feel the weight of the draw and knew it was perfect; this was her bow now and the excitement of having her weapon back in her hands sent a thrill along her skin. Even as she cursed her, she couldn't help but thank Will for refusing to take it.

"I'm afraid this changes nothing," Marian said, her words were gentle and kind, although Robyn could see the pain they inflicted on Alis.

Alis nodded, her mouth held tight in a bitter grimace. "That's just like all you lords and ladies," she shook her head and Robyn was taken aback by the fury of her words, "us lot never understand it when brothers and sons all start killin' each other just 'cause they happen to be princes and kings. But it's when money's involved, that's when you lot change, in't it?" she looked between them accusingly, "Put a price on someone's head and all you lot see is gold."

"Here, lass, there's a bit more to it than that," Littlejohn was calm, he leaned heavily on his stave and his whole countenance was weighed down with more than just his bulk, "it's a matter of trust. We put our trust in this young lass and she let us down. This ain't the first time we've awoken to find she's thieved." He let out a sigh and rubbed his head, "Though I'll admit, I were more prepared first time around." He glanced at Robyn before continuing. "We helped her, she stole from us, she got caught. Then we helped her, and it looks like she stole from us and got caught. We'd have to be daft in the head to put our necks on the line to help that lass again."

"Then she'll be hanged." Alis didn't shout or scream, she simply let the statement float on the air as Littlejohn and Marian exchanged an uncomfortable glance and turned to Robyn.

Robyn realised then that she had the final say. It was up to her to make the decision. To leave Wilfreda to be condemned and somehow persuade Alis it was the right thing to do or... what? *Was there really any other option left after the way Will had betrayed them?* But as Robyn twisted her new bow in her hands, there was a question that burned on her mind that she couldn't find an answer to. *Why had Will refused to steal it?*

"When I went after Will, I asked her why she was taking the money. Why was she taking all of it and running away from her friends," Robyn took a deep breath looking at the three of them in turn, "and she told me that she doesn't have any friends, that there is no such thing as loyalty, and that we all have to look out for ourselves because no one will look out for us."

"I can't say I'm surprised," Marian said sadly, although Robyn recognised the hint of 'I told you so' that Marian only ever needed a slight raise of her eyebrows to communicate.

"Aye," Littlejohn nodded, "certainly explains her ways."

"Well," Robyn said firmly, "she was right."

"Robyn!" Marian gasped. "You don't believe that."

"Don't I?" she looked at her dearest, kindest, sweetest friend, who was ready to give another up to the gallows without further thought. "Because it seems that way. And if I just accept that... well then, that is the way that the world is going to stay."

Marian and Littlejohn exchanged a look but neither seemed any the wiser. "What are you saying, Robyn?" Marian asked finally.

"Listen, Marian, all of you," she stepped back from their small gathering and looked to the travelling players who were now fully awake and observing their discussion with as much interest as if they were the audience at one of their own mysteries. "I didn't set out to help anyone except my own kin," she wanted to be honest, she knew that some of them saw her as a hero and even though she had enjoyed it, she'd always known it wasn't really true, "and had my mother never been in trouble, then I would never have set out at all. But the silver we took from the sheriff has helped people, really helped people." Her friends looked at her waiting for her to continue, and even though she was only feeling her way through the words, she knew that everything she was saying was honest and true. "It would be so easy to stop there. To say I'd done enough good for a lifetime and just hide here in the woods or leave for Brittany and stay with my mother." She looked to Marian at that and knew that the desire to run away, which had been so strong only a few minutes before, was gone and she hoped it was gone for good. "But there is so much more to be done, so many more people who we can help and if we turn our backs on them now... well then, the world really is a very dark and lonely place." Robyn looked to the grim-faced Littlejohn and the wide-eyed Alis. "If we leave Will to her fate, then all we do is prove she was right; that when it comes down to it, no one cares."

"You don't have to prove anything to anyone, Robyn," Marian said softly, reaching out and squeezing her arm gently.

"I think I do," she held Marian's startled gaze and shrugged, "I think we all have a duty to prove the world is better than that. Because that's what it will take for the world to *be* better."

There was a long silence, one in which Robyn could almost hear the heavy blow she had landed on the conscience of each of her friends.

"What exactly are you suggesting?" Marian asked slowly.

Robyn tested the perfect new bow in her hands. The weight was balanced. The string was taut. It felt as though a limb she had lost had suddenly grown back.

Robyn was whole once more and it felt good.

"We are going to rescue Will Gamwell."

29

THIEVES' GAMBIT

Robyn was hidden away in the back room of The Blue Boar Inn playing Fox and Geese and waiting for news. The familiar, simply furnished room in the rafters was becoming almost like a second home, although she wasn't sure how Merek felt about the constant interlopers.

She warmed her hands on the low fire in the brazier as she waited for Marian to move one of the little white counters on the linen game board and Littlejohn eagerly attacked the last of the day's vegetable stew. So far, Robyn's little, red 'fox' counter had eaten six of Marian's geese and there was little chance Marian would be able to surround the fox. But she would never back down from a game until the last move had been played and Robyn smiled as she watched Marian intently staring at the scattered pieces and occasionally moving her hand to one counter then retracting it as she second-guessed herself. The warm, glowing light of the fire made her delicate features even more beautiful and Robyn wondered how long it had been since they had been alone together and when the next chance might be.

Robyn tensed as she heard footsteps on the stairs and

they all looked to see Alis emerge, followed by Merek. "Last customer just left," he said. He had the dark circles and pale cheeks of a man who'd worked hard with little sleep.

"What have you heard?" Robyn asked eagerly.

Merek sighed deeply as Alis sat in one of the chairs, seeming crestfallen. "They have been setting up the gallows in the town square," he said, "so it looks like it will be tomorrow..."

"Aye." Alis added, "All the talk abroad is of an 'anging."

"Been a while since we had a good hanging inside the town." Robyn turned and stared at Littlejohn. He shrugged. "It has."

If the execution was to be tomorrow that didn't give them very much time at all. "Do we know what time?"

"Well, it was in years past they would take the condemned from the Sheriff's Hall to St Mary's Church for her last confession-" Littlejohn started.

"Nay," Merek shook his head and wiped his forehead with his cloth, "she's in the dungeon up at the castle."

"The dungeon?" Robyn had only heard stories of the dungeons of Nottingham Castle, made infamous during the anarchy of King Stephen, there were said to be miles of tunnels and grim cells under the town. Some said there were still prisoners down there from before old King Henry's time, breaking in would be near impossible and nothing like freeing Will from the little castle gaol. "Are you certain?"

"Aye," Merek nodded, he looked tired as he leaned on one of the chairs but he had yet to sit down. "Martha's lad let slip. And there are more than fifty new men on duty starting today. Poor boy's first night off in six-month."

"New men?" Robyn shook her head despairingly. *Where had the sheriff acquired new men at such short notice? Why did it have to happen now of all times?* "Well, there will be no castle rescue then." She hadn't really believed that she would be able to try the same trick again so soon, but she was still disappointed and slightly overwhelmed at how much security had tightened around the castle. If they couldn't get Will from inside, they would have to get her once she was outside. "Can we intercept the parade between the castle and the church?"

Merek and Littlejohn looked at one another. "There's some fair places we could lay an ambush," Littlejohn's face tightened into a grimace, "but we'd need more men, and I've not a notion of which route they'd take through the town."

Robyn wasn't sure if his reluctance was due to the enormity of their task or unwillingness to rescue Will. She had to hope they would all step up when the time came but she was still determined to create a plan in which only herself was put at risk. It wasn't fair to expect such sacrifice from them.

"What about the church itself?" Marian asked, looking around. "Can we set a trap for her confession?"

Robyn liked that idea, but before she could speak, Merek sucked in the air between his teeth and shook his head. "We'll have no help from the priest, he's the sheriff's man, I'm sure. And this lass of yours, well she's no friend of the Church so he'll not risk his neck for hers."

Robyn nodded grimly; the timeframe was tightening.

Suddenly Alis stood, scraping her chair against the wooden floor. "It's as if you all want to see her hanged."

Merek stared at her open-mouthed. "Nay, lass." He stammered but it was too late.

Alis turned and stalked from the room heading back to the bar. "There's still cleaning to be done," she said and disappeared down the stairs.

Robyn's stomach somersaulted. She knew Alis believed they would all rather watch Will die than risk their own necks to save her and Robyn certainly didn't want any of her friends to suffer further as the result of that scoundrel's actions. But nor did she think Will deserved her fate. It was only by the grace of God and good fortune that she, herself, hadn't been caught and hanged before now. She liked to think that if she were facing the gallows, there would still be someone, somewhere plotting her rescue. Suddenly, the thought of Will sitting alone in a cold dungeon facing the certainty of her own execution filled Robyn's belly with fire. She clenched her fist and stood up, more determined than ever to come up with a plan.

"Right," she said, ignoring Alis' departure and continuing as if there had been no interruption, "So that leaves us with one option; the road between the church and the gallows." Robyn paused looking around. She needed to see her plan laid out if she was going to have a chance of making it work. "Help me clear this," her friends jumped to action, stripping the wooden table of pots, pitchers, game boards and stew. It seemed Alis' words had stung everyone's conscience.

Then Robyn drew two arrows and placed them on the table. "This is the road leading from St Mary's church, here," she placed a jug near the arrowheads to represent the church, "to the gallows they're building in Market Square, here" she placed a bowl face down on the fletcher end of the arrow road.

"High Pavement," Merek informed her.

Robyn nodded her assent and she stared at her simple map, then drew her knife. "There is a short alleyway rounding the corner here, is there not?" She placed her knife down cutting across one of the arrows near the gallows end.

"Aye, that's Middle Hill."

"And another, here," Robyn searched around and grabbed a spoon, placing it on the opposite side to the knife.

"Garners. It's a little ways along," Merek corrected her, pulling the spoon further toward the tips.

Robyn nodded. "Good."

"What's thinking?" Littlejohn asked.

"We cut them off," Robyn replied, staring down at her map "like geese surrounding a fox." She glanced around again, finding a little clay oil bottle, she placed it between the arrows near the jug church. "The parade sets off from St Mary's, and they all march along High Pavement," she moved the little clay bottle along between the arrows as she spoke, "but as soon as the executioner's cart passes Garner's ally," she placed down the bottle, and moved the spoon to cross the path, "we cut off the rest of the parade."

"How?" Marian asked.

Robyn smiled thinking of when she had first met Will. "A stubborn donkey should do it."

"What?"

"I want you to emerge from Garner's alley, with Merek's cart and mule to block the road."

"Why me?" Marian asked a distinct note of fear that made her voice rise in pitch, "It's Merek's mule, the poor creature will be used to him!"

"Because," Robyn took a deep breath; she didn't like admitting this, but it was a simple truth, "the guards will get annoyed at Merek, and likely move him and trample through, but a pretty young maid? I'm betting they will wait; some might even dismount to help and I need you to make a great deal of fuss."

"But," Marian shook her head, "what if I'm recognised, some of the guards have seen me with you before?"

Robyn sucked air in through her teeth. Marian was right; it was a risk but she certainly wasn't as well known as Merek. "You can wear a disguise and perhaps change your voice. They will never suspect that a noble-woman is carting goods to market."

Marian sighed. "And all this play-acting will help us, how?" she pressed, "The executioner's cart will still carry on to the gallows."

"But they won't reach them." Robyn moved her knife across both arrows, blocking the path of the little bottle before it reached the end of the 'road'.

"Another mule?" Marian asked, sitting back with her arms crossed and her eyebrows raised in that manner that said, 'this is utter foolishness, Robyn.'

"If we still had Will's donkey... Then maybe." Robyn racked her brain. *What else could they use to block the path? They still had Jasper and Marian's horse Isolde but what use would they be on their own?*

"Barrels." They all turned to Merek's mother. She was sitting upright on the edge of her bed, bright-eyed, and looking at them with certainty. With a stiff groan, she eased herself up with her cane and hobbled over to the table. She pointed at the knife cutting across the two arrows. "We stack all the barrels we can nab at this corner of the market square and when we see the cart; bang!" She motioned a jab with her stick, "take out supports and them buggers will roll themselves right across t'road. Won't stop 'em for long, mind. But they'll be no getting the cart through."

Robyn stared at her. That could work. But there was just one problem. "Where will we get enough barrels?" She asked.

But in reply, she received a quick thwack to the back of her head. "Don't be daft, lass. This here is a tavern."

Robyn laughed, feeling more than a little 'daft' she nodded and looked to Littlejohn. "What think you?"

He rubbed his beard and took a deep breath, looking to the expectant faces of Merek, his mother, Marian and Robyn. "If we time it right, we might gain a few minutes. The Gamwell lass and maybe one or two guards will be blocked within fifty yards or so o'road." He looked at her and shook his head slowly. "But this is a trap and what we need is an escape."

"That's why I'll be here," Robyn pointed to the table next to the little bottle, "waiting for the cart. By the time I've freed Will and handed her a sword, or two, it'll be too late for them to do anything about it." Robyn grinned, seeing her plan come together. "The rest of you can slip into the crowd, so even if the sheriff's men work out you were involved, they won't know who you are or where you've gone."

She looked around at the grim faces of all her friends; Marian winced as their eyes met. "There is an awful lot that could go wrong, Robyn."

Robyn's heart sank. She needed them to believe in her plan and she realised that she needed them to believe in it because she lacked conviction in it herself. She had to admit the truth; there was no use hiding behind false hope. She bit her lip. "There is," she said with a sigh, "but, right now, it's all we've got. So, unless we can come up with something else now, we need to start preparing for this." She looked around her strange little ensemble, a woodsman, a barkeep and his mother and a noblewoman. It wasn't an army but it was all she had and, even with stakes this high, she wouldn't change them for the world.

Her friends exchanged glances before finally Littlejohn sighed and nodded. "Let us hope this goes as well as you think."

"It will," Robyn replied with a firm nod and a grin, praying that she wasn't about to be proven wrong for the final time.

30

MARKET SQUARE

Robyn could see her breath on the air and hoped that the promised rain never materialised. Today needed to be calm and clear. Perhaps a little overcast, but not wet enough for any of their trails to be followed. There was just too much at stake.

Whatever saints were listening, she prayed to them and wondered if there was a saint for lawbreakers and outlaws whom she could ask for benevolence.

Robyn was the last to arrive. It had been tense waiting most of the morning knowing there was little she could do to help the others; the last thing she needed was to be recognised and caught before the day had even begun.

Everyone was arriving to set up for the daily market and were already serving their first customers. She hoped that one more hunched and hooded figure with a long, bulky sack slung across their back wouldn't raise an eye.

She wished she'd thought of a better way to conceal her bow. Simply under a long cloak would have done it. The awkward package kept rolling off her shoulder as she walked and every few paces she would have to swing it back again muttering curses to herself.

But as she came to Nottingham Gate, for the first time she was glad of it; two over-enthusiastic soldiers were checking people who entered. Not discerning enough to check everyone but bored enough to do a thorough job of those they picked out.

Robyn slowed, keeping a careful eye on the two men. She knew one of them by sight. Her breath stopped in her chest. It was the young man with the white beard. The man who'd given chase in the woods, twice. He had been one of the bishop's men then, but he was in the Nottingham livery now. Why was he here? If he picked her out he would know who she was instantly.

Everything would be over and no doubt she would be joining Will on the gallows.

She hesitated. *Should she go through with this?*
"You!"
Her heart stopped. The guard was looking her way.

But to her eternal relief, it was someone else he stepped forward and grabbed. A beggar. She knew him. Nathaniel, poor man, had lost a leg and his livelihood with it. She'd given him a few coins once, but he'd refused to take more than suited his immediate needs.

Nathaniel threw a disinterested wave at the guards with his free hand and shook his head hobbling away with his crutch through the gates as his eager pup yelped at his side.

"We said 'You'." The ex-bishop's man reached out grabbing the cloth of the beggar's haggard old tunic and Nate shook them off.

Robyn hesitated. They shouldn't treat him that way. But if she intervened then she would be recognised, and now was the perfect time to head through the gates unseen.

There was no choice. She turned and hurried into Nottingham. She would remember to thank Nate later for distracting the guards, whether he had known that's what he was doing or not. She just hoped he didn't get himself into too much trouble.

The town was bustling, she tried to keep her hooded head low, but at the same time she was glancing furtively about, she enjoyed the sights and smells of the market and managed to visit more now that she was an outlaw than she ever had when she was a noblewoman.

She recognised Rhys, the Welsh butcher, a portly man with not a hair left on his head. He winked when he saw Robyn and went to offer her a cut of beef but she waved him a 'no'. She couldn't take any gifts today.

As well as the usual bustle and noise of haggling, gossiping, shouting for trade, and managing beasts, a dull hammering filled the air around Market Square. As Robyn rounded the glovemakers stall, busy now that there was a cold snap, she saw the reason for the pounding. The gallows were being finished.

A simple wooden platform with a single high beam running the length of it. As she watched, one of the craftsmen was finishing attaching the ropes. The sight sent a chill right through to her bones.

Somehow, it had still felt like a game until then. While Will was out of Robyn's sight, it was almost as if she was out of danger. But now, on this clear, crisp day, Robyn was watching men putting the finishing touches to the device that would kill someone she still considered a friend. Despite everything.

Her rescue plan had seemed so simple as she talked it through in Merek's back room with the others. But now that she was standing in Nottingham town, everything seemed so much bigger, busier and more real than she remembered. The muddy streets were narrower and filled with so many more people rushing around, there were baskets overflowing with winter vegetables, donkeys and mules heaving wagons, and carts filled with bolts of woollen cloth, and stacks of firewood.

There was so much more going on and so much more that could go wrong.

Robyn shook her doubts away and hurried away from the square as she heard St Mary's bell striking the quarter to the hour. If everything went to plan then Will would never even set foot on that platform.

She decided to check everyone was in place. Even though she couldn't risk being seen talking to her friends, lest they all be linked to the same plot by astute observers, she could still make sure they were both in place.

It didn't take her too many moments to spot the giant of a man and his pile of precariously placed barrels. Littlejohn stood at the corner of Market Square and Middle Hill, casually looking about him as if he was nothing but idleness itself. They had spent the quiet hours of the night before filling Merek's empty barrels with water from the well and heaving them into place, ready to fall on cue. As soon as the first few guards, and hopefully, the sheriff himself, had entered the square from High Pavement, those barrels would 'accidentally' be let loose and tumble down across the road blocking access by cart. No doubt the Guards would curse and swear and set about clearing the barrels quickly but if Robyn had any say in it; they would not be quick enough.

She shuffled past Littlejohn, catching his eye and nodding mildly in greeting as she moved onto High Pavement. The main road leading into Nottingham square from the church was lined with the older Saxon long halls. With their good, strong, timber frames and thatched roofs still fine even now. They were the buildings of alderman councils and guilds, as well as the old Sheriff's Hall where the county court was usually held.

Robyn moved down the road a little, searching for the opening to the alleyway. It was a little way off, fifty yards or so, at the corner of a two-storey building that looked like it might be the merchants' guild. She peered around the building into the alley Merek had called 'Garners'. A mule-led cart, piled high with crates, was parked just a few yards up. The driver was wrapped in layers with a hood covering their face, it was difficult to tell who was under there.

"Morning," Robyn said heartily enough to be heard.

"Aye, mornin'," came the gruff reply of Marian attempting to disguise her voice. Robyn hoped that when the time came, Marian would reveal at least some of her face and make a good attempt appearing to be a damsel in deep distress.

Robyn stood at the corner of the road, looking about. This is where she would stay and lay in wait for the executioner's cart to trundle past. The moment it did, she would signal to Marian.

As soon as the road was blocked she would be free to leap forward and rescue Will. Her pack contained her bow and three battered old swords. They would be enough.

As long as she could free Will before they were both taken down.

Would Wilfreda be in manacles or ropes? She hadn't thought. She wouldn't have a key to manacles. Would she have time to pick the lock? No, of course, she wouldn't. Even if she did, she didn't have Will's lock picks. If the prisoner was in manacles they were done for.

Robyn took a deep breath; it was just another part of the convoluted plan that could go wrong. They still had time to walk away. Perhaps the others had been right.

But the thought of leaving Will to hang made her shake her doubts away. If Will deserved to hang then so did she, for she'd committed the same crimes. And so did the bishop for his theft, and so too the sheriff. Most of England should hang. It was only poor fortune and bad favour that had set Will's fate. If justice was so unfair then it was only right that she should step in and try to even the odds a little.

Robyn bent down to appear as if she was adjusting her boot and glanced backwards to Marian. She dearly wanted to amble down the alley and talk to her, if only for a moment. Just to ask if she was well, if she was ready, or if she was nervous.

She could guess the likely answer to all her questions. But that wasn't the point. Even so, she daren't risk it. If they were seen talking beforehand by a passer-by then their plan might later be put together, Marian might be recognised. She was still not declared an outlaw. She was still likely able to go home to Leaford Manor rather than spending a cold winter in the woods. The last thing Robyn wanted was to save Will only to lose Marian. That was not a bargain she was willing to make.

She turned away. Ignoring Marian's presence and watching the street. It wouldn't be long now. But every moment seemed to stretch to an hour.

Robyn went over her escape route. She wished she'd had time to run it already, but she knew the route well enough. They would have to jump a few fences here and there and she was sure there would be some startled chickens along the way. They would have to go through the tanner's yard then, and if she could make it through there without knocking over any of those foul concoctions tanners loved to keep about the place then she would consider that a triumph.

Jasper and Isolde would be waiting where she'd left them, just beyond the tannery and then it would be a case of riding full tilt for the woods. Once they were in Sherwood, there was no finding them.

Robyn nodded to herself, satisfied.

Everything was in place. Everything was ready.

Then she caught sight of Merek, hurrying down the street from the market in her direction. *Why was he here?* She had done all she could to make sure he wouldn't be involved. He was to be far from here, serving ale and mead to his regulars so none of this could be pointed to him. *What did the man think he was doing?*

He scanned the faces of passers-by. He seemed to be looking for someone. Looking for her no doubt.

People were starting to notice. The last thing she needed was a scene.

"Merek?" Robyn hissed, trying to catch only his attention and the ears of no one else. "Merek!" she hissed again.

He spun on his heel and his eyes landed on her. He looked pale. He rushed forward. "Robyn! Thank the Lord, thank the Lord."

"You're not supposed to be here." She looked nervously about hoping no one of note would spot them together.

He shook his head, out of breath. "It's too late," he said, between desperate panting, "one of the guards, he said, just now, in the tavern," he waved a finger back in the direction he had run.

"What is it, Merek? What's happened?" All concern about being spotted subsided, as she tried to decipher his news.

"It's Will Gamwell," he looked at her, his face hollow-cheeked after too many nights without rest, "she refused confession."

A laugh of relief burst from Robyn. "Don't worry yourself, innkeep," She said, patting his shoulder, "We'll rescue her before she meets her maker."

"No, you fool," he shook his head vigorously, his eyes wide with worry, "she's refused confession, they'll be no mass. No mass means no church. They're heading straight to the gallows. They're coming now!"

Robyn felt a chill run through her blood as she realised the consequences of this. "The parade won't pass here." She felt light-headed. She turned to Marian and caught sight of her pale features below her hood. She'd heard everything. Robyn grabbed Merek and strode off back to Market Square, clutching her bundle of weapons. "How long do we have?"

Merek's mouth opened to answer but he didn't have to. The parade was coming, bells, horns, drums and shouts filled the square and the merrymakers entered from the road opposite followed shortly by the executioner's cart.

It was too late.

Wilfreda Gamwell had arrived at her execution.

31

AT THE GALLOWS

Robyn watched in horror, as Wilfreda Gamwell, stiff-backed and defiant standing in the wooden cage atop the horse-drawn executioner's cart, was wheeled into the Market Square to jeers, shouts and pelted vegetables. Three guards, all in the red livery with the green cross and crowns of Nottingham, rode either side of the wagon with more leading up behind and front. At least twice as many as Robyn had expected. The parade was led by the Sheriff of Nottingham himself, in a fine, blue surcoat and matching hat, riding alongside the familiar litter of the Bishop of Hereford.

The market was teeming with townsfolk and guards. All thought of buying and selling had been put aside as even the sellers abandoned their stalls in favour of getting a good view of the events. Robyn could barely see what was happening and she knew if she tried to get up higher by standing on crates or boxes then there was a good chance she would be spotted. Part of her wanted to turn away. She wasn't sure she could endure the spectacle. She had no desire to see Will hanged even after all the arguing and betrayals. Yet she felt compelled to bear witness.

Robyn searched around desperately and noticed a spot that struck her as a perfect place to hide and yet witness everything. As the sheriff began reading out Wilfreda's crimes, Robyn ran around the side of one of the old Saxon buildings surrounding the Market Square. She threw her bundle of weaponry high up onto the roof, it slid a little on the sloping thatch then caught and held fast. She glanced around for something she could use to step up, there was nothing and there was no time. She dug her fingers into the thatch and used a wooden beam jutting a little from the wall to give her a foothold, heaving herself up.

Keeping low she edged up to the ridge and peeked over the top. She had a view of the whole square, including the wooden platform for the gallows. A second platform that had been erected as a seating area and was slowly filling up with local nobles, some she recognised and even had considered friends. She wondered if they would be friends now. In the front row, sat the now familiar figure of the Bishop of Hereford, he appeared a little worse for wear and was seated next to the sheriff's wife who Robyn hadn't seen since her great turn of fortunes at the Nottingham tournament. Robyn hadn't much liked the look of her then and today she looked as though she had been forced to swallow a particularly foul dose of witches' brew.

"What say you, the accused?" The sheriff turned to Wilfreda, still locked in her cage and there seemed to be a hint more of compassion than accusation in his tone. "You still have the chance to confess your sins and go to God seeking forgiveness for your crimes."

The crowd stilled at this, every ear straining to hear her repentance.

"And what of the bishop?" Will retorted, "shall he confess?"

There was an audible gasp. Robyn's stomach jolted in surprise and even the sheriff seemed lost for words.

Will continued her assault, turning in her tiny cage to face the seated nobles and point a hand through the wooden bars. "You've stolen more than I could in a lifetime, De Vere, are we to hear your confession?"

Robyn wondered briefly who 'De Vere' was, but from the scandalised expression on the Bishop of Hereford's face, she realised it must be his family name, Will had ignored his clerical rank completely. Robyn crawled higher on the roof, inching closer to the spectacle.

"Order!" the sheriff shouted, "Order!" he screeched, beckoning his guards to do something about the caged woman's outburst. But Will ignored his pleas.

"How about we put you to trial?" Will's voice was packed with fury, she screamed her words and the crowd seemed to be enjoying it, cheering her suggestion of a trial.

"How dare you insult me?" the bishop stood, finally responding now that the crowd were siding against him. He pointed furiously at the sheriff, "Nottingham, do your duty, man!"

Will shook the bars of her cage, as guards rushed to subdue her, fumbling with the lock as she continued. "Trial by duel!" Will shouted, the guards surrounded her but she could still be heard, "I hereby challenge the Bishop of Hereford to trial by duel-" her words were cut off and Robyn realised they must have opened the cage. She couldn't see but she knew they would have struck her or at the very least clamped a hand across her mouth. Either way, Will wasn't silent for long. As she was pulled from the cage she scrambled upwards, clambering onto one of the guard's shoulders in a heaving mass of fists and feet. "I'll fight you!" she screamed at the scandalised bishop, "Tie my right hand behind my back and see who God favours-"

Then she was gone, disappearing under the mass of armed guards as the men struggled to subdue her and guide her around the back of the platform to the steps.

The market square was wild with excitement and high spirits. The noises of the parade began again as whistles, trumpets and drums joined in the whoops and calls of the public.

A hanging should be a subdued affair with the accused repentant and calm, going to their end with dignity and forgiveness. A good hanging meant a good death and promised the accused the chance that they might be spared the horrors of purgatory having been cleansed of their sins on earth.

But what they were witnessing today was pure chaos. Robyn wasn't sure if she ought to be proud or horrified, but the grin that spread across her features at Will's sheer audacity couldn't be suppressed.

"Be silent or be gagged!" the sheriff called, directing his order at what seemed like a dozen-armed creature ascending the stairs. He waved some of the guardsmen away until Will was held in place by just two. She was no longer grappling with them and looked at the sheriff but said nothing. He seemed to take that as her acquiescence and turned back to the crowd to formally declare her sentence.

Will was defiant but even from across the square Robyn could see her staring out at the crowd as if she hadn't realised there would be so many. She seemed to be searching the faces for someone and Robyn realised she was searching for someone, anyone, she knew. Will was looking for her. The realisation twisted in her stomach.

What could she do?

Without any kind of a plan formed in her mind, Robyn unwrapped the bow from its leather pack and drew out the quiver. *What would she shoot? The guardsmen? They were just doing their jobs. She glanced across at the man in a black hood, standing on the edge of the platform waiting for his cue. Should she shoot the executioner? That seemed cruel and fruitless; they would simply find another.*

Robyn had thought of a thousand ways her plan would go wrong, but in none of those scenarios had she thought she would end up a helpless spectator.

There had to be something she could do.

The sheriff left the platform, his duty complete and Will was handed over to the executioner, subdued and still. It seemed she had accepted her fate and walked with the black-hooded man toward the noose.

Then suddenly, Will dashed away. The executioner lunged to retrieve her but she was lithe and quick and escaped his grasp. The crowd let out an almighty roar of cheers, laughter, whoops and brays.

It was over in an instant. There was nowhere for her to run but she made the man work for his supper. He grabbed Will's arm, which was small as a twig snatched in his great black gauntlets and pulled her back. But there was no subduing her. He was forced to grab her around the waist, lifting her like a barrel of mead, as he carried her to the stool below the swinging rope.

The crowd cheered, jeered and booed. They hated to see criminals refuse to take their punishment, but they also loved a good scrap and a good show and they especially loved to see the Nottingham guardsmen struggle.

As the executioner tried to place Will down, she lifted

her legs into the air, refusing and clawing at his arms. The poor man could barely see, she was pulling at his hood.

Robyn could hear nothing over the crowd's laughter and cheers but he must have called for help, for two more men ran forward. Will may have been able to cause trouble for one, but with two holding her in place and a third readying the noose there was little more she could do.

Robyn felt a swell of pride in seeing Will fight, but a cold sweat ran across her back; she knew Will was fighting a losing battle.

She pulled an arrow loose from her quiver. She'd made sure to bring non-barbed arrowheads, short bodkins that could penetrate armour and were more likely to leave a bad bruise or a clean wound than the barbed heads she hunted with. A vivid memory flashed in her mind of the ferociously angry Theobald de Lacy wrenching a curved broadhead from a shoulder wound. She shook her head and breathed hard, fighting down an urge to throw up. *Should she kill those men to try and free Will?*

Everything had gone so wrong.

Robyn had clear shots over the crowd. She could aim for the guard's throats. She may even be able to strike all three men down before anyone found her. But to what end?

Three men would be dead and she would be dragged through the baying crowd to hang alongside Will.

There was no choice. She had to stay her hand.

She would have to leave; she couldn't watch Will die. Not when she was so damned helpless and alone yet fighting still. But Robyn was frozen to the spot, her eyes fixed on her friend and an arrow nocked and waiting for its master to decide on their mark.

Will's arms and legs were bound with one long rope that was hastily twisted around her body, as finally, the three men got her onto the stool with her head stuffed through the noose. Any moment now it would be over but Will Gamwell was far from defeated.

"Long live Robyn Hood!" The shout was clear and rang out above the baying bellowing masses.

Robyn's stomach tightened. *Why would she say that? Why would Will use her last breath to mock her? Did Will even know she was there?*

But to Robyn's utter astonishment, almost immediately a group of strong but scattered voices from the crowd replied to Will's call.

"Long live Robyn Hood!" they cried.

"Long live Robyn Hood!" Will repeated her rallying cry and the guards, initially startled into confusion, now sprang into action, leaping off the platform to help the executioner tighten the rope.

But this time the crowd was louder and clearer as more voices joined in the reply.

"Long live Robyn Hood!" Will shouted again.

"Long live Robyn Hood!" The crowd was exuberant. Hats were spinning in the air, women were crying out in high pitched screams, men were bellowing, and everyone everywhere seemed to be banging pots or drums or barrels. No doubt this would go down as one of the best hangings in Nottingham and, as determined as Robyn was, her hope of saving Will was diminishing with every passing moment.

The rope tightened. Will was forced onto her tiptoes as it strained at her neck.

This was Robyn's last chance to walk away but she knew her decision had already been made and she was about to commit the bravest and most foolish act of her life.

Robyn raised her bow and aimed her arrow at the tiniest

mark she had ever attempted. It was a mark that swung this way and that as Will Gamwell fought for her life.

"Long live-" Will was cut off as the stool was pushed from under her feet.

Time had just run out.

Robyn held her breath then released.

32

OUTNUMBERED

Will crashed to the wooden platform and landed hard on her face. She gulped in the air. The noose was still tight around her neck but she could breathe.

Winded and bruised, she rolled onto her back, twisting and turning to loosen the accursed ropes those fools had wrapped around her. She wondered what saint or demon had stepped in to release her from certain death and looked about. But there was only the startled executioner bearing down on her.

He would have her hoisted back up and swinging by the neck in moments.

She wriggled, desperate to free herself from the ropes, but they were too damned tight. All Will could do was manoeuvre her body, shuffling away from the executioner as if she were a caterpillar making for the edge of the platform.

Just as the executioner drew close enough to grab her, she kicked out catching him in the stomach with both legs. He stumbled back. But only slightly and when she went to try again, he was ready. He grabbed one of her feet and although she twisted and raged at him, there was no getting free. She was done for.

A mighty roar came from behind her and a beast of a man sailed on to the high platform plunging feet first right into the executioner's chest.

The poor man had no chance and Will gaped as she watched Littlejohn scramble to his feet and look about. His only weapon was the stave he'd used to pole vault onto the platform. But quick as a flash of lightning he drew the sword of the moaning executioner, turned to Will, slit a single rope and then threw down the sword next to her.

She didn't have to be told twice.

Finally shaking off those damnable ropes, Will grabbed the sword and leapt to her feet, joining Littlejohn in dealing with an assault of guards sent to take them down.

The gallows platform was the ideal place to defend; too high to clamber onto and only a narrow set of steps giving access. This meant they could focus all their attention on one place.

Littlejohn dealt a head swipe to the first guard who ran up the stairs, followed by a hard blow to the chest of the next man. The pair tumbled backwards toppling a third guard and all landing in a heap.

"What's the plan?" Will shouted over the frenzied crowd. She couldn't tell if they were for her or against her but right now, she didn't care.

"Plan?" Littlejohn asked, glancing at her. "Plan were to get you out afore you reached gallows." He turned back to deal with the next assault of heavy guardsmen rushing the steps.

"It's going well then?" She landed a firm kick to the heavy helmet of a guard attempting to clamber onto the platform from below. Then turned just in time to blindly parry a strike. The guard was startled and she swiftly disarmed him then took the chance to swipe him across the chest. He leapt back and landed a little too close to the platform edge. His arms spun wildly as Will lunged, sending him tumbling backwards over the edge and into the baying crowd.

Littlejohn was in trouble. He was fending off three guards at once; parrying attacks masterfully but falling back as he did so.

Will grabbed the last guard's abandoned sword and rushed to join the fray with two blades whirling.

"Where's Robyn?" she asked, panting as she landed a heavy kick to the first guard's knee. He grunted heavily and she used the pommel of her sword to uppercut him.

"Don't know," Littlejohn replied through gritted teeth, as he disarmed another man, bringing down his stave so hard on the man's elbow there was an audible crack and the man screamed.

But Littlejohn was too slow to parry the third man.

Will was too far, and could only scream, "Lookout!" As the guard lunged forward to jab at Littlejohn's side. But the man didn't make the hit. Instead, he screamed and recoiled, clutching an arrow firmly lodged in his shoulder. Littlejohn made the most of the opening and body-slammed the wounded guard who somersaulted as he left the platform's edge.

Littlejohn grinned. "I guess Robyn ain't far."

Elated, they both turned to the narrow steps and halted. Another dozen men were ready to pounce and the man leading the way was at least seven feet tall and nearly as broad, he carried a mace in one hand and a short sword in the other. His heavy helmet hung low over his eyes and his rounded, bare cheeks held a grim smile.

Will knew that even if they managed to take him down, they would still be swarmed by the other guards. It looked as though she would die today after all. At least she would go down fighting.

"Ready?" Littlejohn asked.

"Ready," Will replied, and charged.

ROBYN WATCHED, HELPLESS AS WILL PLUMMETED TO the hard wooden platform. Her arrow had severed the rope, but what now?

Hurriedly, she nocked another arrow as she scanned Market Square for her next target; she had only a minute or so before they discovered her position. She would have to make the most of what she had.

The sheriff was on his feet, pointing and yelling orders, she could silence him in one shot. But the man wasn't wearing armour; the arrow would kill him. Even at this distance. She couldn't do it.

Instead, she plucked a guard from the crowd. He was running along the far side of the square, heading to the platform. She aimed for his armoured flank and he went down like a sack of bricks tripping the men who followed.

"There's the archer!"

Robyn heard the cry, but she paid no heed, her eye was drawn by a giant figure using a stave as a pole vault to leap onto the platform.

"Good man," she whispered, with a nod of awed satisfaction.

A second later both Littlejohn and Will were on their feet and taking down men left and right.

Her arrow aimed here and there but her friends moved too fast and she risked catching one of them by mistake.

First three men were attacking Littlejohn, then two, then just one. The final guard sidestepped, manoeuvring to Littlejohn's unprotected right then lunged.

Robyn saw her chance. In an instant, she aimed and released.

Metal clanged overhead.

Robyn didn't even see if her arrow landed. She spun around to see two blades crossed overhead as Marian deflected a blow headed straight for Robyn's back. A guard had found her but Marian had got there just in time.

It took Robyn a split second to react. She kicked the guard behind his knee and he collapsed, clutching the thatch to prevent himself from sliding off the roof. Robyn didn't wait, she swung herself over the ridge and slid down the other side.

"Come on, Mare!" she called back as she tumbled to the ground and just barely managed to land on her feet.

She spun to look behind her expecting to see Marian in hot pursuit, but instead she was still at the apex. The wretch of a man had grasped at one of her plaits wrenching her backward as she went to escape.

Robyn had her bow up and arrow aimed in flash, releasing an arrow right into the man's heavily armoured chest just as Marian cut through her hair. It was enough to send the man careening backwards with a cry. Marian plunged down the slope and into the waiting arms of Robyn almost knocking her off her feet.

"Are you alright?" Robyn asked, breathless.

"Yes, I've got another set, come on."

It took Robyn a moment to realise that Marian was talking about her plaits as if she hadn't just been in a death-defying sword fight on a roof. She almost laughed, but there was no time for japes.

Ducking and diving, the pair weaved through the thronging crowd. There were cheers and laughter, children had been hauled up to stand on their parent's shoulders, cheering on the marvellous brawl taking place on the 'stage'. Robyn was certain that the travelling players would be jealous of the drama that was unfolding and she was desperate to see how her friends fared.

They dashed past a brewster's market stall, dozens of barrels surrounded a trestle table crammed with tankards and goblets.

"Mare, hold up," Robyn said as she leapt onto one of the barrels, unnoticed by the preoccupied stallholder.

Will and Littlejohn were back-to-back. Will had her two blades and Littlejohn's stave twirled and jabbed. But the fierce pair were surrounded and most of their attention was focused on a man as tall as Littlejohn and twice as wide, who wielded a terrifying-looking mace in one hand and a sword in the other.

Robyn held her breath as she watched and nocked an arrow as the fighters weaved around one another.

The crowd gasped as the mace clanged on Will's second sword. The chain wrapped around the blade and with one tug the weapon was yanked from Will's grasp.

That was Robyn's moment. In the instant the giant raised his prize, Robyn released. The arrow caught the man under his arm no doubt piercing his mail. He cried out and turned to the crowd.

"The archer!" Several voices shouted at once. Robyn leapt off the barrel, ducking into the crowd. But it was too late, she had been spotted and the crowd parted before her clearing a path right across the square to the platform. There were now two dramas unfolding.

Even wounded, the giant posed a threat. But before either of her friends could capitalise on her shot, he leapt from the platform down into the square. Robyn would have sworn on a Bible that the earth shook when he landed.

Marian stood her ground, her sword ready and Robyn nocked an arrow. The giant spun his mace in a protective arc around his chest and head, daring her to shoot again.

If that spinning mace got close enough to strike, then she was dead. Two layers of cloth was no protection against a ball of metal spikes wielded with the strength of an ox. She lowered her bow, a universal signal that she was accepting defeat.

The giant grinned and took a step forward.

Robyn shot.

The giant roared in pain as the arrow struck his foot. He stumbled back and almost lost his grip on his weapons. As he flailed, a flash of red leapt from the platform, landing squarely on his back.

Will grabbed hold of the giant with one hand around his neck and, as the mace came hurtling toward her, she raised her remaining sword. The chain wound around her blade but Will refused to release her grip.

"Come on!" Marian cried, darting forward to take on the giant and snapping the dumbfounded Robyn into action. She fumbled to ready another arrow as the giant fought to steal Will's sword.

But as Robyn raised the arrow to shoot, she couldn't find a clear shot. Marian lunged and the giant parried adroitly even with his left-handed blade and was somehow still light on his feet despite the weight of an enemy on his back.

Marian sidestepped left then right as Robyn struggled to

find a clear target. Then there was an almighty clang as the giant's sheer strength disarmed Marian. Her sword clattered to the ground just as the giant freed his mace, disarming Will. He stood before Marian with two weapons ready to strike her down.

Robyn dashed forward pushing Marian clear and bracing for the weapon's impact.

The giant let out a gurgled screech.

Robyn dared to glance up.

The giant was strangled. A rope dug into the flesh of his neck and Will swung on the broken end of her noose where the arrow had cut through. The giant dropped his weapons grasping for his throat as his knees buckled. He fell backwards just as Will landed and dashed out of the way of his crashing frame.

The giant rolled onto his stomach. Reaching for his dropped weapons and scrambling to his feet. At that moment, Littlejohn yelled, diving from the high platform and landing, with a roar, right on top of the man's back.

It was over.

Robyn breathed in relief as the crowd cheered the finale.

She looked up taking in the faces surrounding her in Market Square. And that was when Robyn realised that the fight was over; but the day had not been won.

More than two dozen guards encircled them creating a six-foot-high wall of armed and armoured men. The lower halves of the men's faces were impassive under their dark, low helmets.

Robyn panted. Her breath only just returning as her friends moved to stand by her side. She scanned the guards for a way through but saw only enemies blocking her path.

The crowd behind the guard-wall parted as a mounted

noble in a fine, blue surcoat and matching hat rode through. He paused just behind his men and leaned forward to take in the remnants of battle.

The dark eyes of the Sheriff of Nottingham looked down at Robyn, almost pityingly as he shook his head and said, "I see it is to be four executions today."

33

LONG LIVE ROBYN HOOD

It was over and she had lost.

Robyn glanced sidelong at Marian. She was pale but fierce and there was fight in her still. There was fight left in all of them. But what could they do?

The two dozen soldiers stood stock still in a circle surrounding the four of them. The crowd, who had been so loud and excitable just moments before, were utterly silent. Robyn could hear the wind rustling the cloth on the market stall tents.

The giant guardsman groaned and clambered to his feet. Littlejohn looked on, gripping his stave so tightly his knuckles were white. None of her friend's made a move and Robyn knew they were waiting for her word. She knew they must be hoping she had some sly and secret plan to get them all out of this. But in truth, she had never intended to put them in the face of such overwhelming danger.

Robyn had gambled all her friends on the life of one and she had lost.

A rotund man in a too-tight burgundy tunic and Phrygian cap stepped between two guards as they moved aside.

She recognised him as the sheriff's bailiff. In lieu of a sheriff's deputy, this man was second-in-command and he had been the one to arrest her mother and spirit away her retinue of servants and tenants. He looked down at her with distaste.

Instinctively Robyn stepped back, but as she did so, her eye was caught by another man stepping into the ring at her right. This man was dressed completely in black even down to the hood that covered his face, only two holes cut for his eyes. The executioner.

"How long before you're ready for them?" The sheriff's barked question startled her.

"Just gimmie a few moments to tie the nooses, sire," the executioner's voice was gravely and he panted while rubbing his chest as though it pained him. Although Robyn couldn't see his face under the black hood, she suspected he was wincing. "It'll be my pleasure."

Robyn's mind whirred. *She could run. Take her chances by darting through the line of men. Shoot one and make a break for it. But would she get through the crowd before she was caught? Would any of her friends make it? Would Marian still be alive by the end of it? Should she go down fighting rather than be hanged? Or give in and plead for mercy? For a trial at least?*

This couldn't be how it ended.

"Let it be known," the sheriff shouted, addressing the crowd and turning to look back at the platform of seated nobles, "That the Nottingham Guard have finally apprehended the murderous outlaw; Robyn Hood!"

Robyn's stomach twisted at her name and a cheer went up from the crowd but her eyes were fixed on the seated nobles the sheriff had addressed. One in particular, the dark eyed woman in burgundy seated next to the bishop. Robyn knew her to be the sheriff's wife and she returned Robyn's stare with such a look of satisfaction and hatred that it made her insides turn to ice.

If there was anything in her life she had ever been afraid of, it was nothing compared to that woman's contempt.

Robyn knew, with a certainty that went as deep as her bones, that there was no mercy to be found in those quarters.

Robyn was dead and she had condemned her friends to die along with her.

"Gimmie that," a voice next to her demanded, the bailiff held out his hand expectantly but Robyn only clutched the handle of her bow tighter.

"Never," she snarled in reply.

Perhaps it was the fear at finally being caught, perhaps it was the sight of so much fighting already today, perhaps it was simply that she did not like to lose, whatever it was, as soon as she refused the bailiff, something compelled her to throw a hard punch, cracking his jaw.

He stumbled back startled and yelping. But Robyn knew she'd damaged her hand more than she'd damaged his face and winced in barely suppressed agony.

"Long live Robyn Hood!" The sudden shout startled her. Robyn tore her eyes away from the bailiff, turning to find the source of the outburst. But as soon as she did the cheer was repeated, this time she recognised Merek, but there were more voices that joined him. Then more.

"Silence!" The sheriff screamed. But the rapturous cheers that followed couldn't be halted by the sheriff's mere commands.

The bailiff made a grab for her bow and Robyn grappled with him expecting to be overwhelmed by guards in seconds.

But they never came. She looked around, still fighting to hold onto her weapon and realised that none of the guards could step-in; they were too busy holding back the crowd. With their arms linked and heels dug in, it was all the men could do to stay standing.

"Silence!" The sheriff cried again as his horse reared in a panic.

But the cry kept repeating. "Long live Robyn Hood!" And the crowd kept pushing forward.

With renewed energy, Robyn twisted the bow from the bailiff's grasp almost falling backwards, but before he could move forward a sword was at his throat.

"What now, Robyn?" Marian hissed her question without taking her eyes from the bailiff.

Littlejohn and Will had taken on the executioner and the giant, and although they might win, the crowd was still pushing forward. The guards were doing their level best to hold back the tide but would soon fall. The sheriff had gone but his horse was still there and Robyn wondered if that meant he had fallen and was now crushed under the stampede. Exactly the fate they all faced as soon as the wall of guards fell.

Then Robyn knew that was the only way out.

Picking out a single guard from the line she almost wanted to apologise for what she was about to do. Instead, she stepped forward and landed a single sharp kick to the side of his knee.

He yelped as his body twisted and buckled, giving into the crush. Wide eyed locals suddenly fell forward on top of him as Robyn leapt back watching the whole line of guards crumble around them.

"Come on!" She grabbed Marian's hand and set off,

calling out to Littlejohn and Will as she leapt over the fallen bodies and forced herself into the crowd.

Shoulders and elbows pushed at her as the crowd of people moved together like an ocean. The relief of the wall of guards falling had made a little room but the gap was almost instantly filled by a new swell.

Robyn forced and pushed and muttered apologies as she weaved through the crowd getting jabbed and struck and elbowed more times than she could count. She didn't know where she was heading but squeezed Marian's hand tight unwilling to let her go for a second.

She glanced back and behind Marian was Littlejohn, head and shoulders above most people, he was a clear target but the crowd seemed to part for him and she was glad he had followed.

Suddenly her wrist was grabbed. She looked to her attacker, ready to fight. But her body relaxed as she saw the friendly face of Merek, pale and beckoning for her to follow.

It was only a few yards to the edge of Market Square but even as the crush thinned it took them long minutes to navigate through. All the time Robyn's eyes darted here and there looking for the tell-tale flash of red with a green cross and crowns that signified the Nottingham livery.

At last they could breathe freely again as they dashed away from the fray, even as more excited and curious newcomers ran toward it. As they followed Merek onto High Pavement, a sudden thought struck Robyn. She paused, let go of her friends and sped off in the other direction.

"Don't wait!" she called as she darted off toward a pile of barrels even as Marian shouted after her.

Robyn found what she was looking for and kicked away the

wooden support underneath a pile of barrels so high it towered over her. The first barrel stayed in place for a long moment until Robyn gave it a good kick and suddenly it tumbled away from the stack taking dozens and dozens with it. She turned and ran back to her startled friends leaving the crash of the barrels to block the road behind them hampering any pursuit.

"I said 'don't wait'!" she cried beckoning them all to keep running as she caught up with her startled friends.

But as she charged past them, running at full speed along High Pavement and away from Market Square, Robyn suddenly skidded to a halt. A horse galloped into her path from one of the side roads and reared as the experienced rider pulled it to a dead stop to avoid careening into her.

Robyn looked up at the mounted guard and her stomach went cold. She knew that face.

Decked out in the Nottingham livery where he'd once worn the livery of the Bishop of Hereford, Robyn recognised the white-bearded man she'd fought and let live in Sherwood Forest a few days before. He peered down at her under the ridge of his heavy, metal helmet.

He recognised her. That much she could tell. As his eyes darted from Marian, to Will and then back to Robyn, she knew he recognised them as well.

"Is there a problem?" Another rider in the Nottingham livery caught up with the first and Robyn realised there was a contingent of at least six heavily armed cavalrymen riding toward Market Square.

Robyn stepped back, slowly drawing an arrow as the white-bearded man's eyes bore into her.

"No." He snapped suddenly, turning to the other man, "Come on," he ordered, then tapped his horse's haunches taking off at a gallop toward the fray behind her.

"What just happened?" Marian asked, panting heavily as they watched the riders leave.

Robyn leaned over and clutched her knees fighting to get her breath back and certain she would never recover from the day's turmoil. "I think," she said, finally feeling the pain of the fight, "that means we won."

"Not yet you haven't," Merek said, gesturing at them to follow him down a side alley, "Let's get you out of here."

34

LONG LIVE THE KING

After changing, bathing, ensuring none of his trampled bones were broken, finding a poultice to deal with the bruise rapidly emerging on his right cheekbone, and dealing with the final business transaction of the day, William de Wendenal had no further excuses to delay.

He took a deep breath and stepped through the large, wooden door into the great hall of Nottingham Castle. The room was cold and badly in need of a good fire, only a handful of candles had been lit as the remaining servants were still on strict orders to keep expenditure to a minimum, and the only three figures in the room were shrouded in shadow.

Maud was stiff backed and silent, seated on one of the long benches, and no doubt cursing every moment of William's delay. Across from her stood a rigid, unreadable attendant and his seated charge, the last man William wanted to deal with, the Bishop of Hereford.

William offered a stiff smile and bowed. "Good evening, your grace."

"You took long enough, didn't you?" The bishop's voice was thick with cold and he looked worse than William felt. His eyes were red and his cheeks for once were pale, he sneezed heavily into a kerchief, and pulled a heavy, woollen blanket tighter around his shoulders as he clutched at a clay bottle, no doubt filled with hot water. He looked in a sorry state.

"Apologies," William replied. Not feeling apologetic in the slightest. "I see you could not resist returning to my exquisite hospitality."

The bishop narrowed his watery eyes. "Less of your cheek Nottingham, I'll have you know your forests are crawling with bandits and I can no longer pay for an escort."

"The king's forests," William quickly corrected, "and the king's forests are patrolled by the king's foresters if I am not mistaken?"

"You know damned well the king's foresters are on holy crusade."

"Which must be why the king's forests are now crawling with bandits, it is a terrible shame that in the king's absence his own lands have been overrun."

"There's no need to be so damnably obtuse about it Nottingham, you've bought all my men and I expect you to put them to good use while you're still in charge. If you demonstrated anything today in that utter shambles of an execution, it's that you cannot be trusted."

William suppressed a smile and did his best to nod solemnly. The bishop was right about one thing; the day had been a disaster but it was almost worth it knowing how furious it made the man. "I understand, your grace, and you are welcome to stay here as my guest until then."

"Stay?" the bishop growled, "I wouldn't stay in this

castle if it was the last island after the deluge. You are a devil, Nottingham. The devil's own dog. You have made a mockery of the very laws you were entrusted to keep, you hear?"

"I see, your grace." William nodded carefully, and bowed. It seemed he had closed the door on any hope of an alliance with King Richard's court.

"You will lose your title. You will lose your lands. You will lose control of Nottinghamshire and Derbyshire and your ancestral seat," he paused mid-tirade and looked at William questioningly, "where is your ancestral seat?"

"I am a younger son, your grace."

"Well, you shall lose this place. You shall be left with nothing," spittle formed at the edge of his mouth as he raged, "mark my words I shall be writing to Chancellor Longchamp this very day and I will see it done."

"Yes, your grace."

The bishop seemed to have worn himself out. He sniffed and appeared utterly miserable as he pulled the woollen blanket further around his shoulders. When he spoke again his tone had softened, he sounded exhausted and sick. "I shall stay in town at the Friary until such a time as I am well enough to return to Hereford."

"Of course, your grace." William attempted his most obsequious tone, doing his best to hide an overwhelming concoction of contempt and indifference.

"I expect you to recapture that harpy."

"Yes, your grace." William bowed again and the bishop stared at him hard for a long moment. Then nodded.

It seemed that was the end of the interrogation, for the bishop rose from his chair sniffing and grumbling and shuffled from the drafty hall; his manservant rushed after him and slammed the door behind them.

William laughed slightly and sat in the recently vacated chair tending to his bruised cheek with his poultice. He looked up at the hanging tapestries; old, moth-eaten and made for a far smaller dining hall. He could barely even tell what the scenes were anymore, probably a chase. They were always a chase. He wondered what new scenes he should get to replace them, a feast perhaps? Acrobats? Some hedonistic pagan festival? That would certainly rile the bishop.

"Have you nothing to say for yourself?"

William turned to Maud. She was in full, glorious, ferocious form. Her dark burgundy gown fluttered in the draft from the empty hearth, and despite the rage carved into that sharp line of her jaw and in those wide almost black eyes, her veil and headdress were perfect. Not a ripple of cloth was out of place. He could see why he'd found her so intoxicating all those years ago, knowing even then how wild she could turn. He wondered if he ought to tell her his news now or leave her to rage a while. He smiled gently which only seemed to further enrage her.

"You think this a jest?" she demanded, leaping to her feet.

William shook his head. "No, my love."

"Well, you don't seem to be taking it seriously. That man is the authority, he and Chancellor Longchamp have complete power while that brat of a man-"

"King Richard?"

"Yes, 'King Richard'," she spat the man's name, "that fool of a king is out roving the holy land, leaving fools to kill us all. Meanwhile his brother's favourite will ride in here at any moment and demand that we hand over all the money we don't have." She screamed the last words and he realised she'd obviously given up hiding her anger from the servants. "So, I cannot see what you find so amusing about the thought of losing your title, your income and likely your life! If we cannot pay off the prince, and we cannot sell our loyalty to the king's court, where shall we go? Shall we fall on your sister's benevolence? Perhaps she can hide us in her Abbey gardens? Or perhaps we could return to my father and live in a hovel on his overgrown manor while he no doubt negotiates with our enemies for the best price he can get for our heads. I swear to you William if I have to set foot in that man's presence again, I shall strangle him and every member of his retinue and then I shall kill you for making me do it."

"I don't doubt it," William replied with a warm chuckle that he immediately regretted as fresh pain shot through his cheek.

"Why are you so damnably calm about this, William?" Maud demanded, "That little bitch-pup murdered our boy, and you! You had her within your reach and let her get away!"

"So, are we admitting Robyn Hood is a woman now or is she still a man?"

"Don't change the subject."

He stared at her for a long moment, knowing he couldn't push her much further without risking his neck but he wanted to play just a little more. "I am calm, my dear Maud, because it is of no consequence."

"No consequence?" She looked about ready to conjure hellfire, "Is it of no consequence that we have been humiliated by that guttersnipe outlaw, Hood? That we are about to be stripped of our land and titles by the king's justice? Is it of no consequence that we owe a debt to Prince John that he will no doubt wring from our blood? A debt we have no possible chance of paying-"

"Now that, Maud, is where you are wrong." Before she could rebuke him further, he drew out his hand from the pouch, slung on his belt and tossed her a bright, buttery gold coin.

She snapped it out of the air with the grace and speed of a wildcat. Then stared. "What's this?" she demanded.

He thought for a moment about playing with her, but his mood was too light for his usual dark sarcasm and a grin pulled at his lips. "A single papal florin," he said, "an unintended gift from the bishop's little harpy. Just one of these is worth twenty silver, it will pay the full wages of two guards for a month."

"How many do we have, William?" she spoke the words to him but her eyes were so fixed on the gold piece he wondered for a moment if she might eat it.

"Enough," he replied, "Enough to make this hole of a castle deserving of us, enough to pay for the extra men I've hired to defend this place, enough to buy us a dozen of the finest robes, and..." he stepped forward and closed his hand over hers, the coin held tightly in her fist, "enough to pay our debts and send the prince's man on his merry way."

Maud let out a soft laugh. "So, this means-"

"John will be arriving in England any day now."

"But the Queen Mother?"

"Has left the country."

"So, the path is clear?" Maud's dark eyes widened.

"Before the month is out, there will be no one left in this country who is loyal to Richard, including our friend the bishop." William moved back to his chair and sat easing his exhausted bones. "England is ready for a new king, don't you think, my dear?"

Maud raised the gold piece to the sunlight and her

tongue darted across her lips in a way that made William wonder if she was part dragon. Her smile grew into a satisfied grin. "King Richard is dead," she whispered, "Long live King John."

35

WILL SCARLET

Robyn arrived back at the abandoned camp and circled it carefully looking about. It seemed she was the first to arrive. She dismounted Jasper giving him a grateful pat.

"You did good," she whispered, trying to temper her nerves.

They'd had to split up. A group of four was too easy to track, and they had each gone off in different directions agreeing to take a roundabout route to throw off any pursuit. But it meant she now had a long and nervous wait for her friends, possibly even the whole night. She would be forced to sit and wait alone, trying not to imagine the scenarios in which each one was captured. Or killed.

"Robyn?"

She spun around at the hushed whisper. It was Marian, hiding in the shadows, just beyond the clearing, staring at her with her blue, round eyes, her hair loose and dishevelled where she'd cast aside the remains of her troublesome decorative plaits.

Robyn opened her mouth to speak but her relief was all-consuming. There were simply no words. All she could do was dash forward and sweep Marian up in her arms. Her heart pounded in her chest as Marian showered her with a thousand kisses on cheeks, forehead, eyes and finally her lips.

Robyn replaced Marian on the ground sliding her arms around her tighter, pulling her deeper into the kiss and almost forgetting to breathe until they finally parted lips, giggling and breathless. They kissed again, fleeting and giddy, then Marian laughed softly, staring up at Robyn with those gentle blue eyes. She reached up to stroke Robyn's cheek and the touch sent an excited shiver across Robyn's skin.

"We made it!" Marian whispered excitedly as if it was a secret just between them, and for a few moments at least, there was no one else in the world.

But all too soon the worry crept back into her mind. "Did you see anything of the others?" Robyn asked.

"Not after we split up to find horses."

But just then, Robyn heard the familiar sound of galloping drawing close to their meeting point.

"Quickly," she said, heading for the bushes that surrounded the clearing, "in here."

Clutching one another in the shadows, the pair lay down low, watching for the arrival, hoping their fears were unfounded. Long seconds passed as the galloping drew closer and Robyn was sure now it was a single horse. But as she moved to leave their cover, Marian yanked her back, with a look of 'don't you dare' on her brow.

But they only had to wait a few moments longer before a weary looking carthorse bolted into the clearing with a scarlet robed rider. Will was desperately trying to gain control of the beast and had only an old rope for a bridle and no hint of a saddle.

Robyn rushed forward, closely followed by Marian, as Will finally calmed the animal, and managed to slide off. She seemed as weary as her mount, as she struggled to stand and turned to Robyn with a laugh on her lips.

"You're alive," she said, catching her breath as her horse nickered and snorted.

"As are you," Robyn replied with a grin and she stepped forward taking her friend into a hug and was surprised at how tightly Will hugged her back. "Were you followed?" Robyn asked pulling back, all this would be for nothing if one of them had led the town guard right here.

Will nodded. "I was, for at least three miles west. I had to shake them off and come back along the river, thank the Lord for low tide, I made this poor lad's feet very wet, didn't I?" She rubbed her stolen horse behind the ear.

"I'm glad you're safe," Robyn said with a deep breath and a smile.

There was a moment of silence as Will struggled to say something, she opened and closed her mouth a few times, and kept her eyes firmly focused on the horse.

Robyn glanced at Marian but she shrugged, closing the gap between her and Robyn and sliding a hand around Robyn's waist.

"What you did back there, Robyn, it was..." but Will trailed off.

"Nothing," Robyn replied quickly, waving Will away and feeling her cheeks reddening.

"It was completely mad." Will turned to her, shaking her head and staring at Robyn with a look on her face that was somewhere between admiration and disbelief.

Robyn grinned. "You're welcome," she replied, with a bow of her head, "Did you see anything of Littlejohn?"

Will shook her head. "No, not after he found me this lad."

"Robyn?" Marian said suddenly, her eyes were wide and Robyn realised why.

There was a pounding of hooves so close there was no time to hide. Robyn spun around and froze at the sight of a fine horse in the livery of Nottingham charging into the clearing. But, almost instantly, she rushed forward to greet Littlejohn as he leapt off the guard's horse with a grin.

"God's wounds," he muttered, noticing a crossbow bolt lodged in his stave and pulling it free, "that one were close. Let me breathe, let me breathe lassies!" He shook off all three women as they rushed to hug him all at once.

"It's good to see you safe, Reynold. You were a true hero back there," Marian patted him on the arm and he grinned warmly at her through his beard.

"Aye, well, I did what anyone would."

"You flew to the rescue," Robyn broke in enthusiastically, "it was like watching an avenging angel!" She remembered her astonishment at Littlejohn pole-vaulting from the crowd onto the platform.

"More like a ruddy great barn owl," he replied.

Robyn snorted. "That too."

"So, where to next?" Marian asked. "Surely we can't stay here?"

"You're right there," Littlejohn replied, "We'll have to move on to a new part of the woods, they shall search round these parts with a fine-toothed comb."

"Can we not just stay at The Blue Boar?" Will asked.

"Can you imagine us traipsing our muddy boots all the

way back t'Merek?" Littlejohn said, shaking his head, "Poor man just got rid of us lot!"

"We could have a barrel each and live out the back," Robyn suggested, and Littlejohn threw his head back in a mighty roar of laughter.

"Long as he don't put us on tap!" he added in between guffaws.

"Sealing you in a barrel is not such a bad idea," Marian said, and Robyn looked at her with exaggerated shock, "It might stop you running headlong into danger for half a minute," she added pulling Robyn back toward her and once again slipping a welcome arm around her waist.

Robyn grinned and pulled Marian closer. "I seem to remember you being right behind me every time."

"Yes," Marian replied, her voice deadpan, "that's what worries me the most."

Everyone laughed at that, and Robyn was so relieved to be alive and back with her friends, the last thing she wanted to do was head off on another chase.

"We can rest our bones here a while at least," Littlejohn suggested, moving toward the logs placed around the long cold fire. As he moved to ease himself to the ground, he kicked something in the leaf matter with his boot and pulled out a bottle. "Look!" he announced with the grin of a little boy given a plum pudding, "Leftovers!"

"Should we be drinking?" Marian asked.

"If we can't drink to victory, Mare, when can we drink?" Robyn replied.

"There's me girl," Littlejohn said, tossing her one of the dozens of cups that still lay abandoned around their camp. "I'd say we got a day or so afore they've searched along the road far enough to find this place," he winked at Marian, "sit yourself down, lass, and enjoy the fact we're still alive."

"You're quite right," she said, arranging herself neatly on a log and wiping around the inside of her own cup with the skirts of her gown before holding it out for Littlejohn.

"Long live Robyn Hood!" Littlejohn said, as soon as all their cups were full to the brim with dark red wine. Will and Marian raised their cups in salute and went to repeat his toast.

"No, no, no," Robyn interrupted with a wave of her hand; if they had proven anything today it was that she was nothing without her friends. "Long live all of us!" She stood, raising her cup and looking at each of them in turn.

"Aye, that's a toast I can drink to!" Littlejohn said as he joined her on her feet and the other two followed with a cheer.

The wine was a little bitter and far too cold. Yet it was possibly the best thing Robyn had ever tasted. They were alive, they had rescued Will, they had turned the starkest odds on their heads, and, once again, they had beaten the Sheriff of Nottingham. Although Robyn was beginning to wonder if perhaps it was not the man's wife that she ought to be more concerned about.

"Where will you go now?" Will asked, breaking Robyn's chain of thought.

"I often heard rumours of an abandoned hillfort some miles west," Littlejohn said thoughtfully, "not been lived in since, oh, since King Stephen's day, I'd say. We could hunt that down."

"You won't leave Nottinghamshire?"

"No," Robyn grinned, glancing at Littlejohn as she sat back down on the log, "we'll stay close enough to cause trouble, won't we?"

"Aye, I'll drink to that." The giant of a man emptied his

cup and promptly filled it again as he rested on the forest floor leaning back against the log.

"And you'll stay close, won't you, Mare?" Robyn asked, squeezing Marian's waist.

"I think I'll have to pay my parents a visit, just so they know I'm alive," her voice drifted as she thought but then her eyes turned back to Robyn and she added in a firmer tone, "but that is not an invitation to ignore me."

Robyn laughed and held her tight. "Don't worry, Mare. I've learned my lesson well," she kissed Marian gently on the forehead, "and I shall endeavour to appear at your window each night with a lute and sing you a ballad to help you to sleep."

"Yes, well," Marian narrowed her eyes, "I think I could do without that." Her frown dissolved into a smile and she turned to Will who sat across from them staring down at her cup. "What will you do now? Where will you go?"

Will looked up. She supped her wine for a moment and then took a deep breath shaking her head. "I'm not sure," she said. "I've no safe-house and I'm certain that, since the hue and cry has gone up, every churchman and layman in the land will be out searching for me..."

"I know how that feels," Robyn said, raising her cup in salute.

"Also," Will added, "I have no coin to pay my way."

"And as I recall," Robyn replied, "You owe me quite a bit of money."

"Well, if we are going to play that game," Will replied with an eyebrow raised, "then as *I* recall, you owe me quite a bit of money as well."

"And how do you work that out?"

"I seem to recall being strung up from a tree not too far

from here while two ruffians searched through my belongings."

"Did you really?" Marian scolded, jabbing Robyn in the side.

"From a tree, Marian," Will repeated with emphasis, pointing at a nearby branch with her cup while Robyn stifled a laugh.

"Belongings you'd thieved," Littlejohn pointed out, pouring out the last of the wine and looking around hopefully for more.

"Aye," Robyn agreed, saluting him with her half-empty cup, "And who was it who saved your neck today?" she asked, turning back to Will.

"Then it looks like both of us owe the other a debt." Will drew her cup to her lips but she couldn't conceal the smirk and Robyn laughed.

"Then I suppose we shall have to stay in one another's company until our debts are paid."

Will looked around at each of them and shrugged, reminding Robyn of a disdainful cat. "I could do worse."

Robyn grinned and put out her free hand knowing that was the closest thing to an admission of gratitude that Will could manage. "Welcome to Sherwood, Will Gamwell."

"No," Will shook her head looking at Robyn's outstretched hand, "No, I don't like that name. I-" Will looked up at her again, those bright green eyes glistened, "I don't want to be her anymore. If that makes sense?"

Robyn thought about her own name, Robyn Fitzwarren, and realised that her given name no longer felt like it fit her anymore either. She was Robyn Hood now and understood exactly how Will felt. She nodded. "Yes, it does."

"Will Scafflocke?" Littlejohn suggested. But Will rejected that name with a grimace.

"Clorinda, Queen of the Shepherdesses?" Robyn suggested standing and announcing the name with a dramatic boom.

"That's *my* false name!" Marian protested, pulling Robyn back down to sit next to her and leaning her head on Robyn's shoulder.

"And a beautiful name it is too," Robyn replied, beaming down at her.

"How about Scarlet?" Will said, thumbing the edge of her vivid red tunic.

Robyn smiled; she liked the sound of that. "Good choice," she said, holding out her hand once more and this time, her friend took it. "Welcome to Sherwood, Will Scarlet."

THE END

DOWNLOADABLE GLOSSARY

'Scarlet' is first and foremost a tale of adventure. But being set nearly a thousand years ago, I wanted to ensure that the 'flavour' of that time-period came across.

As a result, there may be words and phrases within the book that you are unfamiliar with. I have compiled an extensive glossary of the terms used within the text, including some of the more interesting words and phrases, details about the historical characters and their roles (including Robyn, Littlejohn, and Marian), and even a few anachronisms here and there!

If you would like a copy, and learn more about the series, just visit AuthorNiamh.com/RobynHood

ABOUT THE AUTHOR

Niamh Murphy is an author of adventure books with lesbian main characters. Her mission is to write exciting and engaging stories with women taking centre stage.

She is passionate about experimenting with different genres and has a fondness for romance, as well as action-adventure. She has written stories with vampires, were-wolves, elves, magic, knights, sorceresses, and witches as well as contemporary and humorous stories, but always with a lesbian protagonist and a romantic element to the tale.

Read more about her, and find exclusive free content, at AuthorNiamh.com

Printed in Great Britain
by Amazon